"You a

Max spoke softly as he strode to where Kiley stood at the perfume counter.

Startled, she turned. "What on earth—" Then her world spun as her feet left the floor and he swept her up in his arms.

Kiley's breath stopped as his fingers curved under the soft swell of her breasts. Tipping her head back to demand an explanation, she caught a glimpse of firm lips before they covered hers. A shiver coursed through her....

A moment later he lifted his head and still holding her, turned and headed for the main doors of the store. Surprised, she grabbed his shoulders, his muscles rippling under her hands. What would his body feel like against her naked skin?

*You're nuts*, she berated herself. *You should be struggling, screaming ... not mentally undressing your abductor!*

**Judith McWilliams** was compelled to write *Satisfaction Guaranteed* because a good friend of hers has a child with learning disabilities. After discovering the many difficulties and prejudices these children face, Judith knew she had a topic that needed to be explored. Having once worked in a department store like Winthrops, she had her setting. Kiley and Max are the product of her wonderful imagination.

Judith, her husband and their four children make their home in Indiana.

## Books by Judith McWilliams

HARLEQUIN TEMPTATION
 78–POLISHED WITH LOVE
103–IN GOOD FAITH
119–SERENDIPITY
160–NO RESERVATIONS
184–HONORABLE INTENTIONS
253–THE ROYAL TREATMENT

# Satisfaction Guaranteed

## JUDITH MCWILLIAMS

## *Harlequin Books*

TORONTO • NEW YORK • LONDON
AMSTERDAM • PARIS • SYDNEY • HAMBURG
STOCKHOLM • ATHENS • TOKYO • MILAN

Published June 1990

ISBN 0-373-25401-6

# 1

"THE RAT!" Kiley Sheridan exclaimed as she stalked through the door of the teachers' lounge. "The unfeeling, shortsighted rat," she sputtered, her brown eyes sparkling with frustrated rage. "I'd like to boil him in oil, or better yet, douse him with honey, stake him to an anthill and let the ants devour him."

"You won't find many man-eating ants in Washington, D.C." Joanne answered, looking up from the geometry papers she was grading. "But if you're willing to settle for cockroaches..." She glanced in distaste at the corner of the room where one was scurrying for cover.

"Wouldn't work." Kiley followed her glance. "Those blasted bugs are so used to people that they'd probably entertain him."

"Oh, is that what we're trying to do here? Entertain people?"

"Don't be snide." Kiley sank down on the frayed chair across from Joanne. "If you had half the problems some of my students have..."

"And if they were one tenth as good as you give them credit for being... Kiley, when are you going to see these kids as they really are, instead of as you want them to be?"

"As they can be. If only they didn't keep running into myopic twits like this..." She gestured impotently with the sheet of paper she was holding.

"I know I'm going to be sorry I asked, but what myopic twit? Has our principal issued another one of his ill-conceived edicts?"

"No. For once Mr. Beamish isn't responsible. This poison-pen letter is from the head of personnel over at Winthrops department stores. It's to inform me that 'upon reflection I have decided that hiring your students would not be in the best interests of Winthrops,'" she read from the letter.

"Rather a sweeping condemnation, although when I think of some of the kids in your third hour class..." Joanne shuddered.

"I know." Kiley sighed. "A couple of them even scare me, but they're in the distinct minority. Most of my students are basically good kids that our modern system of education has failed to reach. And what's much more frightening is that in another twenty years they won't be a minority. Do you realize that almost half the adult American population can't read a newspaper today?"

"I know, but what do you expect Winthrops to do about it?"

"Provide jobs—provide more than dead-end, minimum-wage, menial work, which is all my students usually get. Winthrops has real jobs with benefits, profit sharing, an in-house day-care center and, most of all, a chance for advancement. For a career. In a few weeks twenty-seven students from my senior level learning disabled class will be graduating. Most of them have minimal skills and almost no chance of landing a good job on their own."

"Kiley," Joanne said seriously, "that's not your worry. The school board hired you to teach underachievers. Period. Once they leave your classroom, they're no longer your concern. That's what we have a guidance office for."

"No, we have a guidance office for kids likes the ones in your math classes. Kids who are going on to college and need help with admission and financial aid applications. The guidance office doesn't have the time, the personnel, the experience or even the desire to help my students."

"All right." Joanne threw up her hands. "I admit it. It may not be fair, but this school is heavily biased toward the traditional student. And I'll tell you what else isn't fair—you aren't going to change the situation."

"I have no intention of wasting my time trying. I know a dead horse when I see one." Kiley absently twisted a strand of short brown hair around a slender forefinger. "I figure the best place to attack the problem is to find some of them jobs, and that's what I've been trying to do for the past three months. It may be trite, but it's true: nothing breeds success like success.

If I could just place a few of them..." She gazed blindly out the window.

"I don't like that look on your face," Joanne said wryly. "The last time you looked like that was when you threatened to go to the newspapers if Mr. Beamish took part of the cost of a new tackling dummy for the football team out of your supply budget. I remember what an uproar that caused. The football coach still won't speak to you. It's a good thing you've got tenure or you'd be history."

"I may be persistent, but I'm not stupid."

"Persistent, hell! You're plain pigheaded, but from the sound of things, you've met your match in what's-his-name there." Joanne nodded toward the letter still clutched in Kiley's hand.

"Tom Preston, and you may be right," Kiley admitted. "But if I could get my kids into Winthrops then other businesses might reconsider. It looks like I'll have to try someone else at the store."

"Who? I thought you said this Preston character is the head of personnel."

"Of personnel, but not of the store." Kiley's eyes narrowed thoughtfully. "That honor belongs to Max Winthrop."

"Forget it," Joanne advised. "I was reading an article the other day about how he took over Winthrops when his father died eight years ago and turned it from a static performer into a thriving, expanding chain of department stores that stretches from here to Boston."

"He sounds like a man with vision, which is exactly what I need."

"What you need is a good, healthy dose of common sense." Joanne eyed her with resignation. "You haven't got a chance of convincing Winthrop to hire your students. He's—wait a second, I'll show you." Joanne got to her feet and began to rummage through the stack of dog-eared magazines on the table beside the coffeepot.

"Here!" She triumphantly extracted a tattered local Washington magazine and, finding the article she wanted, shoved it at Kiley.

"That's Max Winthrop?" Kiley's eyes widened as she stared at a full-page picture of a man who had just pulled himself out of the turquoise pool behind him. His wet, ebony hair was slicked back, his bright blue eyes gleamed with laughter and his firm lips were parted in a grin that exposed perfect white teeth. Water droplets sparkled like diamonds in the heavy pelt of black hair that covered his broad chest and arrowed down over a flat stomach to disappear into a minuscule pair of white trunks. Masculine charisma positively oozed out of the picture.

"Not someone you'd care to fool around with, is he?" Joanne demanded.

*Oh, I wouldn't say that*, Kiley thought irreverently. *Fooling around with Max Winthrop might be the sensual experience of a lifetime.* He looked like the embodiment of her every wicked fantasy.

But it was what was inside the magnificent physique that was important, she reminded herself. If he really was as good a businessman as Joanne seemed to think, then he was probably also arrogant, ruthless and highly pragmatic. Not at all the type of man to appeal to her. Or to agree to give her kids a chance.

Kiley grimaced. "Max Winthrop is not going to be easy to convince."

"But you're still going to try?"

"I have to," Kiley said simply. "No one else seems willing to. But thanks for showing me the article. You know the old saying, forewarned is forearmed."

"Funny, the old saying that springs to my mind is there's none so blind as he who will not see. Kiley, you're thirty-three years old. When are you going to realize you can't change the system single-handedly?"

"Which brings us to yet another old saying." Kiley grinned at her friend. "Where there's life, there's hope."

"Of all the—" The bell signaling a class change suddenly rang, interrupting Joanne's rebuttal. With a resigned sigh, she returned to her papers as Kiley hurried out, intent on reaching her classroom before her fifth-period students arrived.

BY SATURDAY MORNING, Kiley had decided that the best way to approach Max Winthrop was to go directly to his office and talk her way into seeing him. If she tried to make an appointment she'd have to state her reason, then he'd undoubtedly check with his personnel manager who would prejudice him against her cause.

Kiley sighed as she reached for her eye makeup. She didn't like simply showing up on his doorstep. It smacked of unprofessionalism, but, as much as she'd worried around the problem in her mind, she hadn't been able to come up with an alternate plan. It wasn't as if they had any mutual acquaintances who could introduce them. She grimaced. Max Winthrop moved so far outside her social circle that he might as well be on another planet.

She added a final touch of liner to her eyelids and stepped back to view herself in the full-length mirror on her bathroom door. She'd put a great deal of thought into what to wear and she'd finally decided to dress as if she were a successful businesswoman, hoping the image would make him feel at ease with her.

The problem was that she had never had any real contact with the business world, so she wasn't sure exactly what a successful businesswoman would be likely to wear to a Saturday morning meeting. She'd bought a book specifically written for women trying to compete in the business world and had followed its recommendations exactly, purchasing a tan linen suit in a slightly more conservative style than she normally favored.

And the results weren't bad, she decided, checking the restrained shine on her best Italian leather shoes. Picking up the matching purse, she glanced at her

watch. Nine-fifty. Perfect. She should reach Winthrops main store on Wisconsin Avenue at ten forty-
five. Late enough that he should have already dealt with
any problems that might have come up when the store
opened and still too early for him to have left for lunch.

"AND HARRY WANTS YOUR FEEDBACK on the sketches he
sent you for the Christmas window displays. They're
on your desk on the right-hand corner. Under that pile
of junk from the Stanford Alumni Association."

"You might be the perfect secretary, Aggie, but your
values are askew. The mailing from Stanford isn't junk.
What's junk are Harry's sketches. He actually wants to
use high-tech laser holiday scenes for our windows!"
Max impatiently ran his fingers through his crisp black
hair. "Whatever happened to Santa Claus and Ru-
dolph the red-nosed reindeer?"

"Max!" Bill Damos, the head of advertising, burst
into the office.

"Whatever happened to knocking?" Aggie shook her
graying head in annoyance.

"This is an emergency," Bill excused himself. "A disaster."

"Everything's a disaster with you." Aggie sniffed
disparagingly. "I'll get busy on these letters, Max." She
sailed out of the office, closing the door behind her.

"Calm down and give me the gory details, Bill," Max
said soothingly.

"Ryan Smithson was on his way to the store when his taxi had to brake suddenly and he was flung against the door handle. He broke his arm and blackened his eye." Bill delivered the information in tones of deepest gloom.

"Unfortunate," Max said, "but hardly a disaster. The store will still be here when your friend is healed."

"He isn't my friend. He's an actor we hired."

"*We* hired?" Max asked with a frown. "What did we want with an actor?"

"As part of the promotion of that new perfume we're featuring. Remember I mentioned at the staff meeting last week that my contact at one of the local television news shows had agreed to send out a cameraman to film it. He's going to air it tonight right before they sign off. You know, in that twenty second slot where they show something that's happening around the metropolitan area."

"Oh, yes. Now I remember. The idea you billed as every woman's fantasy—being swept off her feet and carried away by a tall, dark stranger. I take it the fantasy demands physical perfection?" Max's eyes twinkled.

"This isn't funny!" Bill wailed. "What are we going to do?"

"Well, look on the bright side. At least your Mr. Smithson won't have to worry about getting a hernia to go with his broken arm."

"Will you be serious, Max!"

"I am being serious. Contrary to fiction, modern women are heavy and modern men are notoriously out of shape."

"You aren't, you're . . ." Bill's voice trailed away, and his pale blue eyes began to gleam.

"No!" Max had no trouble interpreting the gleam. "Absolutely, unequivocally no."

"Max, listen to me. We picked Smithson specifically because he looked like the popular conception of a high-powered business executive. You're the real thing and you look it. Pure silk tie in a nice, restrained burgundy, spotless white shirt, a three thousand dollar gray suit with vest and handmade shoes. It's a shame you're only five foot eleven," Bill lamented. "Smithson was six foot four. But you can't have everything."

"You can't have anything, my friend."

"Max, it'll be easy. All you have to do is walk up to the female model who'll be standing by the perfume counter, sniff the air around her, sweep her up in your arms, kiss her, carry her out through the main doors, tenderly deposit her into the waiting antique Mercedes convertible and drive off into the sunset."

"Drive off to the nearest psychiatric ward would be more appropriate," Max snipped.

"Max, you've got to help. The female model's already in place and the cameraman's secreted behind the counter so that he won't draw a crowd. Not only that, but I bragged about this promo being on tonight's news show at the retailers' luncheon yesterday. If I can't pull it off, I'll be a laughingstock."

Max eyed his dejected-looking advertising executive with a certain amount of sympathy. Bill was right. He would take a lot of ribbing for failing to deliver after his big buildup. And it wasn't Bill's fault. He could hardly have foreseen a traffic mishap. Max frowned as he realized that the store would also come in for its share of ridicule.

"What about Wesley from personnel?" Max suggested. "He certainly fits the stereotype of masculine beauty. And he's over six foot."

"He's got a bad back, and besides, his taste in clothes doesn't fit the image. Max, you're my only hope." Bill eyed him with a pleading expression that reminded Max of the cocker spaniel his parents had given him for his sixth birthday.

"Oh, all right." Max conceded defeat. "I'll do it. But if you ever come up with another harebrained advertising stunt . . ."

"Never again," Bill lied. "I've learned my lesson."

"So, how do I recognize this model I'm supposed to abscond with?"

"Jessie's five foot five, slender, with short brown hair, and she'll be wearing a beige suit. She'll be at the perfume counter. I'll grab a picture of you out of our files to show her so she'll recognize you."

"It'd be better if I had a picture of her," Max pointed out.

"We don't have one. She and Smithson have worked together before so we didn't need it. Don't worry. She'll give you a sign."

"If I believed in signs, I wouldn't be doing this," Max muttered.

"It'll be fine," Bill insisted. "Just give me a five-minute head start to get things moving, then come on down. After all, what can go wrong?"

"What can go wrong!" Max yelled at Bill's back as he left. "Do you want an itemized list or would a general overview do?"

"Just be there as close to ten forty-five as you can," Bill called back.

KILEY PAUSED inside the main entrance of Winthrops and took a deep breath to steady her racing heart. She glanced at the huge ornate clock over the door. Ten forty-two. So far so good, she encouraged herself. Everything was going exactly as she'd planned—except for her nervousness. She swallowed uneasily as her stomach lurched. So much depended on her convincing Max Winthrop to give her students a chance.

A woman hurrying into the store bumped into her, and Kiley automatically moved forward, pausing as she reached one end of the perfume counter. Blindly she stared at the assortment of perfume testers and tried to think.

Maybe she should go to the tearoom and drink a cup of coffee to steady her nerves before she tried to see Max

Winthrop? She glanced at the clock—10:44. No, she'd better not risk it. She might get held up and miss him if he took an early lunch.

Squaring her shoulders, she turned away from the counter toward the elevators and saw Max Winthrop striding down the aisle toward her. Damn! She bit her lip. He was obviously on his way out of the store. She had to stop him. Her students graduated in under two weeks, and time was running out.

As his eye caught hers, she gave him a bright smile and prepared to speak to him. If necessary, she'd grab hold of his suit jacket and force him to listen to her, she thought with a burst of determination.

To her relief it wasn't necessary. He slowed down as he reached her and gave her a searching glance. Assuming he'd mistaken her for someone else, Kiley prepared to take full advantage of the fact.

Slowly she forced her eyes upward, past the soft glow of his silk tie, over the sparkling whiteness of his shirt collar, along the straight column of his tanned neck. Kiley hesitated fractionally as she considered the uncompromising angle of his chin before stopping at the sight of his firm lips. With a fascination that was totally divorced from either her nervousness or the seriousness of her mission, she studied their upward quirk, noting the deeply carved laugh lines beside them—as if he found much in the world to amuse him. Somehow that fact gave her the courage to look higher still, up past his slightly oversized nose, to where she became hopelessly entangled in the most incredible pair of eyes she'd ever seen. They were blue, the bright blue of the Aegean Sea at dawn.

"For once Bill didn't exaggerate," Max murmured so softly she strained to hear him. "You really are unmistakable."

Before Kiley could force her sluggish mind to decide how to use this chance encounter to her advantage, Max, seeming oblivious to the people around them, swept her into his arms and cradled her against his chest.

Tipping her head back to demand an explanation for his extraordinary behavior, she caught a glimpse of his lips a second before they covered hers. The impact scattered her protests like so many dry leaves in the wind. His mouth felt as firm and warm as it had looked, and she was unable to suppress the sudden shiver that shafted through her body. A shiver that quickly became a torrent of sensation as his tongue outlined her lower lip.

Her feeling of disorientation increased as he suddenly began to move, heading toward the front doors of the store. Startled, she grabbed his shoulders. Her bewildered gaze swung over the faces of the Saturday morning shoppers, who were watching the unexpected drama in rapt fascination.

A deep flush reddened the pale ivory of her cheeks as Kiley registered the avid looks of frank envy in the eyes of the women. Of all the embarrassing situations she'd ever found herself in—and her students had involved her in a few real beauts over the years—this one topped them all. Hastily she hid her face against Max's shoulder and tried to distance herself from what was happening. That proved impossible. The faint fragrance of his spicy, masculine cologne confused her senses. The ripple of his chest muscles when he adjusted her weight in his arms as he went through the door a grinning man obligingly held open for him made her wonder what those muscles would feel like without the covering cloak of clothes.

*You're nuts, Kiley Sheridan,* she berated herself. *Absolutely nuts. You should be struggling, screaming, doing something to object to such cavalier treatment, and what are you doing? Mentally undressing your abductor.*

She gasped as Max suddenly deposited her on the brown leather seat of a gorgeous antique convertible.

Why hadn't she objected, she asked herself as she watched Max walk around the long gleaming hood of the car. Because she wasn't afraid. She was embarrassed, confused and intrigued, but not afraid. Not of Max Winthrop.

Everything she'd been able to find out about him—and her homework had been considerable—highlighted the fact that he was an intelligent, purposeful, success-oriented man. He was not a kook. Since he'd picked her up and carried her out of the store, he had a reason. But what? She studied him curiously as he started the car.

Could he have mistaken her for someone else? It hardly seemed likely. Even if he normally wore contacts and wasn't wearing them now, he'd have to have realized his mistake when he'd kissed her. That kiss had been unique—totally distinct from anything she'd ever before shared with a man. But that was no reason to assume it had been as earth-shattering for him. He might experience that tingling, all-encompassing surge of mindless pleasure every time he kissed a woman. The thought unexpectedly depressed her.

Max stopped the car at a red light and said, "Bill forgot to tell me where we're supposed to go after we ride off into the sunset, Jessie."

"Wrong," Kiley said succinctly.

"He did?" Max frowned.

"Being unacquainted with Bill, I wouldn't know. What I do know is that my name is not Jessie."

"Not Jessie!" Max took his foot off the clutch in surprise. The car lurched forward, coughed once and died.

"Dammit!" Max muttered and restarted it. Once clear of Wisconsin Avenue, he swung the car into the first parking spot he found, cut the engine and turned to Kiley.

"You have to be Jessie. You're a gorgeous brunette wearing a light brown suit."

Kiley ignored the warm glow of pleasure she felt in favor of understanding what had happened.

"You can't honestly believe that all brunettes wearing light brown suits are named Jessie?"

"Apparently not even all the gorgeous ones," Max said. "Well, if you aren't Jessie, who are you and why didn't you say something?"

"Say something!" she repeated incredulously. "When was I supposed to say something? When you were kissing me? When you grabbed me like some latter-day Tarzan? The situation was embarrassing enough. All I wanted to do was to get away from all the people staring at me and, since you were headed out the door, I simply went along, Mr. Winthrop."

"Call me Max." His lips lifted in a reluctant grin. "At this point formality would be ridiculous."

It might as well be, Kiley thought ruefully. Everything else seemed to be. "And my name is Kiley. Kiley Sheridan."

"Kiley Sheridan," he repeated slowly. "Well, Kiley, would you mind telling me why you gave me that pleased smile if you aren't Jessie?"

"Is only Jessie allowed to smile at you?" Kiley stalled for time as she tried to decide how to handle the situation. Her original plan of assuming the disguise of a businesswoman seemed to have been dealt a death blow. Perhaps if she could put him on the defensive . . .

"Stop equivocating and give me a few facts."

"Me!" she yelped. "I'm the one who was minding my own business when some male who's seen one too many cowboy movies abducted me. I think I'm the one who's entitled to an explanation."

"But you smiled at me," Max defended himself.

"Thank goodness I didn't speak to you," she said tartly. "The mind boggles at what your reaction might have been. Now, tell me what this is all about."

"We were filming a twenty-second promo for the news tonight. I was supposed to sniff the model's perfume, clasp her to my manly chest, kiss her and carry her off."

"They certainly cast the manly chest right," Kiley muttered then flushed in embarrassment as Max's shout of laughter made her realize she'd inadvertently spoken her thoughts aloud.

"Thank you," he said solemnly. "I like your chest, too."

Ignoring his provocative comment, she tried to follow the logic in what he'd told her. "Since when does the owner of the store do his own modeling?"

"Since he sent his brains out to be aired," Max answered dryly. "You see, five minutes before we were set to go, the male model called from a hospital emergency room to say that he had been in an auto accident and couldn't make it. My advertising director was frantic."

"And so you stepped into the breach?" Kiley's lips twitched. It really was kind of funny. If she hadn't been the victim, it would have been hilarious.

"I didn't see any cameras," she added, trying to understand what had happened.

"The camera was hidden behind the counter. But that still doesn't explain how you recognized me. I know I've never met you," Max persisted.

"No, we haven't met, but I was coming to the store to talk to you."

"Nor was I supposed to see you." Max studied her thoughtfully. "I always check my appointments first thing in the morning."

"Yes, well…I was hoping you'd make time to see me because of the seriousness of the situation." The words came out in a rush.

"Yes?" he said encouragingly.

"I teach the learning disabled at…" Her voice trailed away as his indulgent features hardened.

"And you want my store to take on some of your substandard students," he said flatly. "My personnel director discussed your request with me. He didn't tell me your name."

"My name is irrelevant. My students aren't. They deserve a chance."

"A chance to do what? Create mayhem in my stores? Winthrops has spent a hundred and fifty years building a formidable reputation for service. Your students aren't going to wreck it."

"There's no question of them wrecking anything," she said soothingly. "They simply want good jobs like everyone else. Do you have any idea what some of my kids are up against? The fact that they even want to work at all says something about their tremendous resilience despite overwhelming odds. Easily half of them have been victims since the day they were born. Victims of their parents' inexperience or incompetence, of their apathy and despair. Victims of a social system that threw a welfare check at them then ignored them, and most of all victims of an educational system that wasn't equipped to handle them."

"All right," Max sighed. "I'll admit that there are extenuating circumstances, but since society as a whole created the problem, surely society should be the one to solve it. However, I'd be glad to send a check to—"

"They don't want a handout, they want a *hand up!*" Kiley's voice throbbed with the intensity of her feelings.

A pedestrian on the sidewalk beside the car gave her a startled look and hastily moved away.

"This discussion is pointless," Max insisted. "I've already given you my decision and I'm not going to change it."

Kiley stared at her lap, wishing she was five years old again and could throw a temper tantrum. For the past three months she'd been listening to a steady diet of "no, go away and quit bothering me" from local business people. But the problem wouldn't go away. Come Monday morning she'd be looking at a whole classroom of teenagers who desperately needed help in order to realize their potential. Help that Max Winthrop could give them if she could somehow find the key to unlocking his resistance. But how? She chewed her lip in frustration. How could she make him listen? How could she lure him out from behind his prejudices long enough to consider, really consider, what she was asking him to do?

Unless... She stared blankly at the dashboard. Could she somehow use this morning's mix-up to her advantage? He'd talked about guarding his store's reputation as if it was of vital importance to him. Suppose she threatened to talk to one of the scandal sheets about what had happened? Would the threat of the resulting publicity make him listen to her?

Kiley glanced uncertainly at him. Or might it cause even more problems? Might it not harden his position even further? She studied his firm jawline with misgivings. Max Winthrop would make a dangerous enemy, but she had to take the chance of antagonizing him. This was much too important for her to just give up on. Too many futures were at stake.

"What are you plotting now?" Max glanced at her tense features.

"How I can make you listen to me," she replied honestly.

"Make?" His voice hardened, and Kiley felt a tremor of unease. "As in blackmail?"

"How about gray mail?" She gave him a tentative smile, and encouraged by the slight lift of his lips, continued, "Look at this from my point of view, Max. I'm espousing what I know is an unpopular cause to an unreceptive audience. Just as I know that if you'd listen, really listen, you'd want to help. Do you blame me for using whatever means I can to try to reach you?"

"Even underhanded ones?" He seemed no more than mildly curious.

Kiley released her breath on a long sigh. "No, of course not. I'm not going to try to force you into anything. What I am hoping is that you'll feel you owe me the courtesy of hearing me out after what you just put me through."

"I see." Max started the vintage car and pulled into traffic.

"Where are we going?" Kiley asked curiously.

"My home. I don't think either of us wants to go back to the store until things have died down. And you're right. After this morning, I do owe you a hearing."

"Thank you." Kiley felt almost light-headed with relief. She'd done it. She actually convinced Max Winthrop to listen to her. Now if she could convince him to hire a few of her students. She began to marshal her arguments, wondering which he'd be the most susceptible to. If only she knew more about the business world, she thought in frustration.

# 2

"WHERE DO YOU LIVE?" Kiley asked as they crossed into Virginia.

"McLean. We can talk there without being interrupted. It'll—" he broke off as a speeder, weaving through the heavy traffic, cut in front of them, forcing him to brake suddenly. "You'd better buckle your seat belt."

Kiley glanced at the leather seat and announced, "There isn't one. This car is an antique."

"This car's a moving death trap," Max muttered, moving into the slow lane. "If something happens, put your arms around your head, brace your feet against the floor and crouch over."

"Hmm," Kiley murmured, watching his long tanned fingers as they competently gripped the steering wheel. She felt safe with Max. A feeling she was at a loss to explain. Just as she was at a loss to explain her compulsive attraction to him. It was more than the normal appreciation of a woman for a superbly masculine man. There was something about him that drew her. And it made no sense. She didn't know Max Winthrop well enough to be fascinated by him. So why was she? She shifted uneasily.

"We'll be there shortly. Don't worry." Max caught her movement and misinterpreted its cause.

Twenty minutes later, Max turned between a pair of massive red brick pillars and followed a wide drive-way for about a quarter of a mile before making a sharp right turn that suddenly revealed his home.

Its sheer beauty made Kiley catch her breath. Built of the same red brick as the stone pillars at the en-trance, the house sprawled over a slight rise like a be-nevolent giant. Tall windows with sparkling white frames marched across the two full stories, and a series of dormered windows punctuated the bluish slate roof. Great masses of rhododendrons had been planted around the front of the house, and their glistening green leaves provided a perfect visual contrast to the dull red brick.

Max stopped the car in front of the three shallow brick steps that led to the oversize, black front door. Above the door was a six-foot-high antique fanlight that emphasized the height of the entrance hall.

Max started to insert his key into the gleaming brass lock when the door suddenly swung inward.

Kiley blinked, then blinked again. Subconsciously, she'd been expecting a replica of the perfect English butler. Instead she seemed to be faced with a Beatrix Potter character.

The elderly woman in the doorway barely topped five feet. She was comfortably plump without being fat and was wearing sturdy leather oxfords and an over-long dress covered by a dirt-streaked gardening apron. On her head was a beige straw hat decorated with a profusion of silk flowers.

"Mom!" Max enveloped her in a bear hug. "I wasn't expecting you till the picnic. What brought you down from Maine?"

"Your Uncle Martin."

"Uncle Martin? He's not here. At least, I sure hope he's not."

"I know he's not here. He's at my house. He and that stingy wife of his simply appeared. They said they wanted to see me." She sniffed. "What they really wanted was free room and board on the ocean for two weeks. I stuck it out for four days and then I left them the house and came to visit you. But I didn't expect to see you home so early. And with such a lovely companion." She eyed Kiley with approval.

Kiley smiled tentatively.

"Mom, I'd like you to meet Kiley Sheridan. Kiley, this is my mother, Anthea Winthrop."

"Hello." Kiley held out her hand, hoping her surprise hadn't been apparent. Somehow, she hadn't expected the matriarch of the Winthrop family to look so endearingly eccentric.

"I'm pleased to meet you, my dear." Kiley found her hand grasped in a surprisingly strong grip. "Are you a friend of Max's or a business colleague?"

"Neither, at the moment. I teach the learning disabled at one of the local high schools and I'm hoping that Max will hire some of my students to work in his store."

"Why, Max, what a wonderful idea. And so like your dear father." She gave him a misty smile. "You can't know how happy it makes me to see you following in his footsteps. Why don't you and Kiley go into the library and work out the details while I do some pruning in the rose garden."

"Certainly. If you'll come with me, Kiley?" Max said, and Kiley winced at the ironic note in his voice.

Surreptitiously, she observed him closely as she followed him down the hallway. Had she done her cause any good by inadvertently enlisting Mrs. Winthrop's aid? Max didn't seem to be the kind of man who would take kindly to having his hand forced—even by his mother. Although . . . She remembered the very real pleasure in his voice when he'd greeted Anthea. He obviously loved his mother a great deal. Kiley wondered if Max would indulge his mother and hire her students.

Kiley's musings were interrupted when Max opened the doors to the library. Three inside walls of the impressive room were lined with books while the outside wall had four sets of French doors that opened onto a brick patio filled with white lounge furniture and a vast array of potted flowers. She half turned, catching her reflection in the wavy glass of the antique mirror above the fireplace.

"If you'll have a seat?" Max gestured toward one of the two leather chairs in front of the fireplace and she obediently sank into one.

When he made no attempt to break the silence, Kiley asked, "What exactly did Tom Preston tell you?"

"Tom said that you wanted him to hire kids who couldn't get jobs elsewhere."

"That's not precisely true. Most of these kids already have jobs."

"Then why pester me?"

"Because the jobs they have are dead-end ones. Jobs that are great for earning spending money, but they have no future. Winthrops offers good salaries, benefits and advancement from within," she explained.

"Advancement!" Max snorted. "How can people be promoted when they can't even read?"

"They can read," she said mildly. "Their skills are simply substandard. For a whole variety of reasons, none of which have anything to do with their basic intelligence. Now the six kids I have in mind—"

"Six!"

"Six," Kiley repeated doggedly. "With one exception they all have minimal reading skills, and once they get some positive feedback in the form of job success—"

"What about Winthrops in the meantime? What are my customers supposed to get out of this besides a hassle?"

"Service. And I'm sure once my students actually start their jobs, their reading skills will improve by leaps and bounds."

"I'm afraid I can't share your rather naive optimism. Hasn't it occurred to you that if those kids were the least bit self-motivated they'd already have the needed skills?"

"Not necessarily." Kiley refused to concede the point. She was certain her students would work hard once they had real jobs. "The kids I have in mind all have adequate math skills. There would be no problem with making change."

"Over half our customers use credit cards. You obviously have no idea what's involved."

"What's involved are six lives," she said intensely.

Max stared into her tense face in mounting frustration. Why couldn't she see that what she was asking was impossible? It would make a shambles out of his carefully streamlined work force. Kiley Sheridan had no more understanding of the cutthroat nature of the retailing world than his mother. He sighed, suddenly feeling tired. He hadn't yet managed to convince his mother that sentiment had no place in business and he'd been trying for almost fifteen years. He doubted he could convince Kiley, either, but he had to try. He wanted her to understand that he wasn't being arbitrary or unreasonable but only protecting his company.

"Max, you must have hundreds of employees. Six more can't possibly make that much difference in the long run."

"You're wrong, Kiley. Incompetent employees do make a difference." Max stared out the French doors at the rolling sweep of green lawn. "You know," he continued, "you and my father would have had a lot in common. He could never resist an appeal for help, either. When he simply gave money, it was no problem. Unfortunately, he fell into the habit of offering positions to his friends when they found themselves out of work—usually for good reason. By the time I took over the running of the stores eight years ago, there were so many incompetent people fouling up so many key positions that Winthrops was stagnating. My father's well-meant but ill-conceived desire to help almost cost everyone at Winthrops their livelihood—the competent and the incompetent alike. I swore I'd never fall into that trap."

"I'm not asking you to. What your father did and what I'm asking aren't at all the same," Kiley insisted. "Think a minute. Your father was giving out jobs to friends, which undoubtedly meant well-paying jobs in upper-level management where a high level of competency is essential. My students will be coming in on the ground floor. Nothing they do can affect management decisions."

"Perhaps not," Max said slowly, "but I still say you're thinking with your heart and not your head. You need to see what running a store is really like." Max stopped as if considering an idea. He gave Kiley a steady look as he said, "If you're not busy this afternoon I can show you what I mean."

"I'm free." Kiley forced herself to accept his proposition when what she really wanted to do was to go home and have a good cry. It was depressingly clear that neither her arguments nor his mother's wishes would change his mind. His suggested trip to the store was nothing more than an attempt to justify his refusal to hire her kids. But then she grew hopeful, if only because he felt obliged to explain his position. Max Winthrop had a social conscience he was trying to appease. And, if he had one, there was still the possibility, no matter how remote, that she could reach it. And reach it, she would.

"WHAT'S THE FIRST THING you notice about my staff?" Max asked as they stepped out of the elevator on the sixth floor.

"Well..." Kiley studied a middle-aged saleslady who was helping a woman choose a pair of shoes. From the stack of boxes on the floor beside her, she'd been at it for quite some time. "Patience?" Kiley guessed. "I mean that shoe saleswoman still looks friendly and by now she must be tired."

"Close. The first priority of our clerks is a friendly interest in our customers no matter how provoking they might be. And, believe me, some of them would drive a saint to distraction. Our clerks are here to provide a service and they're trained to never forget it."

"Trained." Kiley jumped on the word. "Your employees aren't born perfect salespeople. They receive training, just like my kids will, when you hire them." She gave him a hopeful smile that sent an inexplicable surge of tenderness through him.

"There's no when about it," he said firmly. As he was forever telling his mother, sentiment had no place in business. "Your kids haven't even got the patience to learn to read."

"It's not patience they lack, it's incentive," she said seriously. "And only one is a nonreader. The rest are simply sublevel. My students are all labeled learning disabled, but that's a catchall phrase. Exactly what it means depends on who you're talking to."

"How so?" Max asked curiously.

"Well, the kids I deal with tend to fall into one of two groups. Those who come from severely deprived social or economic backgrounds and those who suffer from a clearly definable physical limitation that interferes with their learning via traditional methods.

"For example, one of the students I want you to hire is a true dyslexic, and nothing I or anyone else can do is every going to enable him to read. But true dyslexics are extremely rare. I've only seen three in all the years I've been teaching. Usually the child has a much milder form of dyslexia. If it's caught early and the teacher knows what she's doing, the child learns to cope quite well. In fact, by the time the students get to high school they're almost indistinguishable from the general run of the school population. But if the dyslexic child isn't diagnosed and helped early, by the time he gets to me, he's had ten to twelve years of unsuccessful learning. The student thinks of himself as a failure, and I have to overcome all that emotional baggage before I can even start on the problem."

"I take it a lot of physical disabilities aren't detected early?" Max asked, his interest caught.

Kiley sighed. "Not early enough, although when you consider how many overcrowded classrooms there are and add to that a shortage of qualified special education teachers, it's surprising the number isn't larger."

"And you expect me to solve a mess like that by giving some kids a job? Kiley, training has to build on what the person already knows. I wasn't kidding when I said that there's a lot more to working in a department store than simply walking up to people and asking them if you can help them. Suppose a customer wanted to buy a pair of boy's jeans for her daughter. She tells you that her daughter wears a girl's size eight. What size should she buy?"

"An eight?" Kiley guessed.

"Wrong. The salesperson would check a chart at the register that shows size conversions, from boys' to girls', from European sizing to American or the difference between a junior size seven and a miss's size eight.

Come over to the record department and I'll show you another side of the same problem."

He nodded down the aisle to his left.

She glanced around, groaning inwardly as she noticed the avid interest of the two clerks standing behind a nearby cash register. Max Winthrop was clearly an object of intense curiosity among his staff. Although, she thought ruefully, the female segment would probably notice him if he was the janitor. There was something about him . . . Probably his stubbornness, she thought mockingly as she followed him into the extensive record department.

"Listen," he whispered as they approached the counter.

"Yet?" Kiley caught the last word of a question a boy of about sixteen was asking.

"Just a second and I'll check." The clerk reached under the counter and pulled out a blue folder. Opening it, he turned the pages, ran his finger down a list and said, "That record isn't due to be released until July twenty-second. Would you like us to reserve a copy for you?"

"Uh-huh." The boy nodded.

"Then if you'll give me your name and phone number, we'll call you when it comes in."

Max motioned Kiley through a pair of doors labeled Staff Only at the back of the department.

"Now tell me your students can handle that."

"My kids can," Kiley insisted, keeping her doubts to herself. She'd make sure they could handle it if she had to provide tutoring on the side.

"Kiley" Max said wearily, "you aren't looking at the situation clearly."

"At least I've looked. All you've seen is what you want to see."

"I see what is important for the stores," Max corrected.

"All right. I'll admit you've made some valid points. But I have, too. And I came and viewed your situation firsthand, while you're judging my students on the basis of your own prejudices."

"I am not prejudiced!" Max was genuinely shocked by her charge.

"Everybody's prejudiced," she said earnestly. "They're just prejudiced about different things, and your prejudices are tied to what your father did. But before you turn down my kids because of what happened in the past, the very least you can do is view the situation through my eyes."

"You mean through rose-colored glasses?" he asked wryly.

"No, through the classroom. Visit the class that has most of the kids I want you to hire in it. It starts at 10:05 and ends at 10:55. Surely you can spare fifty minutes?" she pleaded.

"What is it about you, Kiley Sheridan?" he asked in exasperation. "I know I'm right and I know I'm not going to change my mind, but . . ."

"You have a conscience?"

"What I think I have is a super saleslady." He eyed her wryly. "You wouldn't happen to want a job, would you?"

"I already have a job."

"No, what you have is a crusade," he said slowly. "And the potential for a great deal of heartache." He gently moved his fingertips over her cheekbone.

Kiley clenched her teeth as the hairs on her cheeks seemed to electrify at his casual touch.

"I . . ." A crash caused by a nervous stockboy in the corner seemed to make Max think better of what he'd been about to say. "Very well, I'll meet you at the high school at ten on Monday."

# 3

"YOU'RE LATE, KILEY," Millie greeted her as she hurried into the principal's office. "The most gorgeous-looking hunk was in here asking for you."

"Was?" Kiley's eyes widened apprehensively. "Didn't he wait? Where'd he go?"

"In there." The secretary nodded toward the door to her left labeled Byron Beamish, Principal. "Our beloved leader took one look at the guy, lit up like a Christmas tree and dragged him into his inner sanctum."

"Drat!" Kiley muttered. That was all she needed. Mr. Beamish would monopolize Max's time with tales of the awards won by his outstanding students. She'd been afraid of Mr. Beamish's interference when she'd asked Max to visit her classroom, but there'd been no way around it. The visitors rule explicitly stated all guests had to sign in at the main office upon arriving at the school. She had no intention of flagrantly breaking it and giving Mr. Beamish a weapon to use against her.

Kiley looked at her watch. The class she wanted Max to observe started in two minutes and she didn't dare leave it unsupervised. There were several students in it who might take advantage of her absence to create havoc. She had no choice but to extricate Max from Mr. Beamish's clutches. She started toward his office door.

"Mr. Beamish said he wasn't to be disturbed," Millie warned.

"Too bad. Max Winthrop is my discovery. Let Mr. Beamish find his own."

"I doubt if you want the guy for the same thing Mr. Beamish does." Millie giggled. "Honest to goodness, Kiley, I didn't think you had it in you to come up with a man like that."

"Mr. Winthrop and I are merely business associates," Kiley corrected her.

"What kind of business? Monkey business?" Millie asked slyly.

Kiley sighed, knowing that by lunchtime news of her supposed romantic involvement with Max would be all over the building. Millie was an inveterate gossip, and what she didn't actually know she was more than willing to make up.

With a perfunctory knock on the principal's door, Kiley opened it and stepped inside. Ignoring the annoyed expression on Mr. Beamish's face, she gave him a polite smile and said, "Thank you for entertaining Mr. Winthrop until I got here, Mr. Beamish."

She turned to Max. "Good morning. It was good of you to come."

Kiley was immediately hit with his vibrant masculinity and she swallowed uneasily. Why did this man affect her so strongly? She'd hoped that her unusual reaction to him had been caused by the strange circumstances of their meeting. Unfortunately, there was more to it than that.

Compulsively, her eyes were drawn to his, and her heart sank at the annoyance she could see shimmering just beneath their brilliant blue surface. For a brief second, she regretted they hadn't met in more normal circumstances without the problem of her students' futures, but then common sense reminded her that if it hadn't been for the kids, she never would have met him.

"But we haven't finished, Miss Sheridan," Mr. Beamish protested. "I was just telling Mr. Winthrop about our advanced calculus class. Four of our students have been accepted by MIT and I'm sure Mr. Winthrop would be interested in meeting them. To say nothing of our Westinghouse Science finalist."

"I'm sure he would have enjoyed meeting them," Kiley said diplomatically, "but he's here today to visit my third period class and if we don't hurry we'll be late."

Max gave Mr. Beamish a polite smile and, taking Kiley's arm, followed her out of the office.

"My classroom is just down the hall." She gestured to their left. "I appreciate your coming."

"I wasn't aware I'd been issued an invitation. I thought it was more in the nature of a command performance," Max said dryly.

"I'm sorry if you feel threatened . . ."

"You're a threat all right," Max muttered and Kiley sighed, refusing to admit even to herself how much she'd wanted him to say that he'd come this morning because he wanted to help her students.

"Tell me," Max asked, "is your principal always like that?"

"Like what?" Kiley asked cautiously.

"Blowing his own horn about how great the school is."

"Mr. Beamish takes a great deal of pride in his students' accomplishments. And he does have a lot to brag about," she added fairly. "Not only do we have a disproportionate number of National Merit finalists for a school our size, but we've also had finalists in two of the last three Westinghouse Science Foundation competitions. And this year, one of the students in the creative writing class placed in the top five of the Avon-Flare novel-writing contest."

"Where does that leave you and your students?" Max asked shrewdly.

She grimaced. "Way out in left field, but in all justice to Mr. Beamish, his performance as a principal is judged on how well his students do. My kids are struggling to reach minimum standards. It isn't really that he's against them. He just doesn't feel that they belong in a traditional high school setting."

Kiley paused in front of her classroom door and turned to Max. "Please remember that I'm not advocating your hiring all these kids. I'm quite willing to admit that some of them are totally beyond the point where a job would help solve their problems."

Kiley jumped back as a wad of paper came flying out the door.

"At least your students are normal in some regards." Max chuckled as he watched the paper hit the wall and fall to the floor.

Kiley stepped into the open doorway. "Good morning, class. We have a visitor this morning." She gestured to Max.

"He from the school board?" a painfully thin girl demanded.

"No, Mr. Winthrop is simply interested in education. If you'll sit there—" she nodded to a seat on the far side of the room well away from the class's main troublemakers "—we'll get started."

Sending up a silent prayer that nothing disastrous would happen in the next fifty minutes, Kiley moved to the front of the room to begin the day's lesson.

A sense of satisfaction filled her. The majority of her students were on their very best behavior in an attempt not to embarrass her in front of her guest. She hoped it was a sign that everything would go well.

Unfortunately, she did not take the principal into account. With only five minutes left in the class, Kiley had completed the day's lesson and was standing by her desk explaining a point in phonetics to one of her students while the rest of the class was going over the next day's assignment. She looked up and saw Mr. Beamish in the doorway.

"Good morning, Mr. Beamish," she said.

"Miss Sheridan." He started into the room then paused, frowning as he noticed what the student in the seat nearest him was doing.

"Miss Sheridan, are you aware that this young man is reading a comic book?"

"I know he's reading, sir." Kiley suppressed her annoyance at his antiquated idea that only a book constituted acceptable reading material.

"He—"

"If you want to read it yourself, you'll have to wait your turn." Max's chuckle seemed to diffuse the principal's anger. "I get it next."

"I see." Mr. Beamish laughed ponderously. "Well, I hope you'll be willing to forgo the treat, because I have some students in my office I'd like you to meet. That is, if you've finished with him, Miss Sheridan?" He shot Kiley a challenging glance.

It was much more likely that he was finished with her, Kiley thought gloomily, but she forced a pleasant smile, knowing that if she hadn't already convinced Max to give her students a chance, five more minutes wasn't going to make any difference.

Kiley studied Max's impassive face as he got to his feet. He looked like the consummate businessman, cool, calm and remote. Especially remote. Her heart sank.

"Thank you for sharing your class with me, Miss Sheridan. I'll be in touch." He gave her a polite smile as he followed the triumphant Mr. Beamish out.

In other words, don't call us, we'll call you, Kiley thought bleakly as she watched him leave.

The jarring sound of the bell shook her out of her state of impotent frustration, and with a tired smile at her departing students, she sank behind her desk. Now what, she wondered as she rubbed her forehead, trying to ignore the tension headache building behind her eyes. She couldn't force Max to hire her students, and even if she could, she wouldn't. An unwilling employer could create intolerable working conditions, and she wanted to help her students, not drive them into a nervous breakdown.

Kiley took a deep breath and tried to look on the bright side. Winthrops wasn't the only employer who suited her purposes, merely the best. When it had taken Tom Preston several months to answer her letters she had begun to contact other businesses, and she still had some names left on the list of possible employers. Surely in an area the size of metropolitan Washington she could find one company willing to give some of her students a chance. She'd prove Max Winthrop wrong.

THAT EVENING, she combed the business section of the paper in an attempt to identify potential employers she had missed. To her dismay she found it difficult to work as Max's lean features kept superimposing themselves on the newspaper. Finally, in frustration she tossed the paper on the coffee table and leaned her head back on the couch.

*Damn that man. Why couldn't she get him out of her mind?* She tried to analyze her reaction. He was good-looking, but she'd dated handsome men without feeling this attraction. He was extremely wealthy, but money had never been important to her. She had an active social life, so it wasn't loneliness. What—

The melodious chime of her doorbell interrupted her thoughts, and grateful for the distraction, she rose and peeked through the long narrow window to the right of the door. Her heartbeat sped up as she saw Max standing on her doorstep. She hurriedly unhooked the chain and swung open the heavy oak door hoping her flushed face wouldn't reveal her inner turmoil.

What was he doing here? Was he going to hire her students? Or did he feel that he owed her a personal explanation of his rejection? The only thing she knew for certain was that she was much more glad to see him than she had any right to be.

"Good evening, Max."

"Kiley. I stopped by on the off chance that you'd be in, but if I've called at an inconvenient time..."

"No, not at all. I was merely doing some long-range planning. Come in and sit down."

Max walked in and looked around approvingly at her bright, spacious living room. "Very nice."

"Thank you," Kiley said, inordinately pleased at the honest admiration in his voice. She'd worked closely with the architect to design her small house. She was very proud of what they'd achieved, and she liked the

way Max looked in her home. "How did you know
where I live?"

"Tom Preston gave me your address." Max continued to survey the room.

Finally, unable to bear the suspense, she took a deep
breath and asked, "Why are you here?"

"I said I'd be in touch."

"People say lots of things," she replied dryly. "What
they mean is something else entirely."

"I'm not people. I'm me. Max Winthrop. And if I say
I'll do something, I do it."

"Why do I get the feeling I've just been threatened?"

"Guilty conscience?"

"Are you going to hire some of my students?" She
went straight to the heart of the matter.

Max walked across her living room, pausing in front
of the sliding patio doors, which led to her flower-filled
deck. He turned, and Kiley blinked as the evening sun
streaming in through the glass doors engulfed his head
in a brilliant halo of light. She blinked again and the il-
lusion vanished. As it should, she thought ruefully.
Max Winthrop was many things, but angelic did not
number among them.

"I've decided to give in to my mother's misguided
pleas and give a few of your protégés a job. Provided
certain conditions are met."

"What kind of conditions?" she asked cautiously.

"Conditions that try to safeguard the reputation of
my store."

"But—"

"No buts. Hiring someone who doesn't meet our minimum qualifications is something I swore I'd never do. Having already given up that much, I fully intend to minimize my risks."

"How?" Kiley asked, not liking what he was saying.

"First of all, we will discuss each person to be hired, with me having the deciding vote."

"Who does this we include?" she asked apprehensively.

"This is strictly between you and me." Max's words were casual, yet there was a curious intensity in his eyes that made her vaguely uneasy. As if there was something she was missing. Telling herself she was being fanciful, she nodded in agreement.

"Second, the hirings are probationary for six months and can be terminated at any time at the store's discretion."

"That sounds extremely arbitrary," Kiley offered tentatively.

"Not really. All new employees have a probationary period."

Kiley's eyes narrowed. "Is six months standard?"

"No, it's usually three months."

"Then why make my kids the exception to the rule?"

"My hiring them is an exception to normal policy, so you can hardly complain if their continued employment also has exceptions."

"Yes, I can, but I won't because it isn't necessary. My students are going to be such great employees you won't want to get rid of them," she declared emphatically, ignoring his skeptical expression. "You said the first condition. What's the second?"

"I have no intention of simply turning them loose in the store to sink or swim on their own, because if they go down, they're likely to take my store's reputation with them," Max replied.

"There are more important things in life than your store's reputation," she said mildly.

"Of course there are, but we aren't discussing our personal philosophies. We're discussing the store, and a business's reputation is a perilous thing at best. Once lost, it's hard to regain."

"All right, they need supervision," Kiley conceded. She didn't entirely agree but this wasn't the time to argue.

"As I see it, your protégés need three things: a sympathetic hand on the reins, instruction in basic math and reading skills and, perhaps most importantly, help in learning how to cope with the customers. That's where you come in."

"Me?" Kiley blinked. "How?"

"As instructor, guidance counselor, mother confessor, whatever is needed."

"I'll be glad to help in any way I can," Kiley assured him.

"Good. I believe school is out for the summer a week from Wednesday?"

"That's right."

"Then, if you'll stop by the store after school one day next week we'll schedule a time for your students to fill out the paperwork necessary to get them on board and I'll show you an office you can use."

"Office?" She frowned. "I hardly need an office to offer occasional advice."

"You're going to be offering a lot more than occasional advice. Not only will you be teaching a class every day, but I want you right there on the spot if a problem comes up. By the time you return to school in the fall, things at the store should be well enough in hand that we can transfer your students to the personnel department."

"I see," Kiley said slowly, taken aback by his high-handed proposal.

"It's a package deal, Kiley." Max stepped in front of her and continued. "You and the kids, or neither."

Kiley closed her eyes and tried to think. Part of her wanted to agree to Max's conditions, and not just because she hoped she could be a real help to her students. The more compelling reason was standing in front of her. The very thought of spending a summer working closely with Max Winthrop sent a rush of excitement through her and that worried her. She was already much too aware of him. And every time she was with him, the feeling seemed to grow.

Despite the fact that Max Winthrop represented a very real threat to her peace of mind, he also represented a tremendous opportunity for her students that she couldn't turn down simply because of what might develop between them.

She stole a quick glance at Max to find him still watching her with an intent expression that gave her pause. Like a predator watching his prey to see which way it was going to jump before pouncing. It's just his business expression, she assured herself. She took a deep breath, knowing there was no real choice involved.

"All right," she agreed, and saw the tension drain from Max's face. She wondered if he had been hoping she'd refuse so that he could scrap the whole idea.

"Good. Since what you'll be doing this summer is basically personnel work, we'll call you a personnel consultant and pay you accordingly."

"No." Kiley shook her head.

"You want to be called something else?"

"What you call me is irrelevant. It's the pay I object to. I won't take money."

"Why not? You'll earn it."

"Because . . ." She faltered, not sure even in her own mind why she didn't want to take money from him. All she knew was that at the moment they were equals. If she started accepting money from him, even though it came through the store, there would be a subtle shift in their relationship. A shift she was certain would be for the worse.

"For several reasons," she finally said. "First, I already have a job that supports me, and second, since you wouldn't have hired me if you weren't hiring my students, it's unreasonable to expect you to pay me, too.

"And, more important," she hurried on when he opened his mouth, "if I accept money from the store, then my loyalty would have to be to the store, and I give you fair warning I'm on the kids' side."

"No!" Max said in mock astonishment. "I would never have guessed that. Tell you what," he continued on a more serious note, "if you promise to tell me if you change your mind, we'll try it your way first."

"All right," Kiley agreed, rather surprised he'd given in so easily.

"Since that's settled, how about if we seal our bargain with a drink?"

"I'd love to." She reached for her purse, missing the gleam of satisfaction that lit Max's eyes.

# 4

"EXCUSE ME," Kiley murmured apologetically as the influx of shoppers crowding into the elevator on the fourth floor pushed her against an elderly lady.

"No problem." The woman smiled at her. "One has to expect a few inconveniences for bargains like this." She nodded toward the bulging shopping bag at her feet. "Winthrops is a great place to shop."

Winthrops is a great place, period, Kiley thought happily. And in less than a week six of her students were going to be part of it. She glanced around the crowded elevator with a proprietary feeling. She felt like urging her fellow passengers to get out and spend more money so Max could afford to hire more of her students.

"Eleventh floor," the elevator's tinny recording announced, and Kiley stepped out.

She paused in the hallway and studied her surroundings as she absently rubbed her rib cage where she'd received a sharp jab from a box someone had been carrying. In contrast to the crowded floors below, a quiet air of serenity permeated here. Assuming that Max would have his office somewhere near Tom Preston's, she headed to her right, away from the credit offices and the beauty salon.

Her surmise proved correct. She stopped in front of a door labeled M. Winthrop and took a deep, steadying breath as her heartbeat accelerated at the thought of seeing Max again. She ran the tip of her tongue over her suddenly dry lips as she remembered how tiny silvery lights burned deep in his brilliant blue eyes.

"May I help you?" a woman's voice asked and Kiley flushed, embarrassed at having been caught standing in front of Max's office door daydreaming about the wretched man. Turning, she gave the woman a bright smile.

"Thank you, but I was simply collecting my thoughts before my appointment with Mr. Winthrop."

"You'd do better to check your life insurance," the woman said candidly. "He's in one hell of a mood."

"Oh?" Kiley frowned.

"Not that I blame him," the woman said judiciously. "It was a frantic day to start with, what with the sale starting, and when you add to that a shoplifter who lost his head and knifed the security guard who apprehended him . . ."

"Someone was stabbed? Here? In the department store?" Kiley's eyes widened. She wondered what she was getting her students into.

"If you knew half of what goes on in this place . . ." The woman shook her head knowingly. "Judith Krantz could set one of her novels here and she wouldn't even have to use her imagination." The sound of a door opening down the hallway interrupted the woman, and with a cheerful grin and a whispered, "Good luck," she stepped into the office behind her.

Refusing to allow the woman's warning to upset her, Kiley pushed open Max's door and stepped inside. She found herself in an elegant room furnished with what looked to be early American antiques. Several floral arrangements in gleaming lead crystal vases had been scattered around the room, adding a warm touch.

Kiley walked to the middle-aged lady who was seated behind an oversize cherry desk typing into a computer. The woman paused, glanced up and gave Kiley a bright, professional smile.

"May I help you?" she asked.

"Yes. I'm Kiley Sheridan here to see Mr. Winthrop."

"So you're the woman who convinced Max to hire those kids that Tom was so set against." She studied Kiley curiously.

"Yup, that's me," Kiley said with determined cheerfulness.

"Don't be annoyed." The woman had caught the flash of emotion in Kiley's eyes. "One of the first things you'll find out is that this store is just like a big, extended family. Everyone is always busily poking their nose into everyone else's business, but there's no malice in it. At least, not usually," she qualified. "By the way, I'm Aggie Brown. Max's—"

"Right hand ma—person." Max emerged from his office in time to interrupt Aggie. "Good afternoon,

Kiley." He gave her a tired smile that unexpectedly tugged at her heart strings.

"Aggie—" he turned to the older woman "—call the floral department and have them run some flowers over to Hastings. He's at the university hospital, room 412. Come in, Kiley."

"I didn't realize that retailing was such a dangerous occupation." She followed him into his office.

"Normally it isn't. Have a seat." Max gestured toward the large leather chair in front of his desk. "In fact, in all the years I've been in retailing, I've never had a shoplifter attack someone before."

Kiley's eyes were drawn to his face. He looked exhausted, and she felt an overpowering urge to rub away the deep lines carved beside his mouth. To cradle his head against her breast and soothe away all his worries.

Determinedly, she banished the tempting thought. Max Winthrop was a business colleague, she reminded herself.

"It makes no sense," Max ran agitated fingers through his hair. "Despite the fact that shoplifters cost American businesses over twenty-five billion dollars a year, even when they're caught, they rarely serve more than a few months. It isn't worth the risk to carry a weapon, let alone use one."

"Maybe your shoplifter was high on something?" Kiley suggested.

"It's certainly possible." Max sighed. "I should have known something like this was going to happen today after the escalator ate that girl's skirt."

"What?" Kiley blinked in confusion.

"Some college kid wearing a very long skirt got the hem caught in the escalator between the fifth and sixth floors and instead of calling for help so that a sales clerk could stop the escalator she kept trying to yank the material free."

"So what happened?" Kiley asked curiously.

"The escalator was stronger. It ripped her skirt off."

"Good Lord! What'd the poor soul do?"

"Got off at the next floor and calmly wrapped herself in the nearest thing at hand, which was a man's bathrobe."

Kiley shook her head in bemusement. "The most exciting thing that ever happened to me when I went shopping was that I overspent my budget."

She'd look great in a man's bathrobe, Max thought. With her gleaming brown hair tousled, her full lips kissed bare of the clear red lipstick that now coated them, her soft brown eyes languorous and a warm flush heating the delicate ivory of her cheekbones. She was such an intense advocate for those students of hers, throwing her whole being into what he very much feared was going to be a hopeless cause. Would she bring that same intensity and single-mindedness to other aspects of her life—like making love? He shifted uneasily as he felt his body react to his thoughts.

"Um, about my students you're going to hire?" she asked, wondering what had caused the abstracted expression on his face.

"Yes, your students." Max forced his mind to the reason for her visit. "What are my choices?"

"I brought a list of the six most likely candidates," she said carefully. "I would prefer it if we didn't interview a large group and then reject all but six of them. These kids don't need that. Most of them have already faced enough rejection in their lives."

"I see. Well, we can try it your way. Suppose you— Damn! What with everything else going on today I forgot to take the measurements, and some of the staff are bound to leave early since they were in early because of the sale," he said in exasperation.

"Whose measurements?" Kiley scrambled to follow his sudden change of topic.

"Not whose. What's." Max rifled through a stack of papers on his desk, extracted a small notepad and, taking a tape measure out of his desk drawer, got to his feet.

"We'll discuss your kids while I take care of it." He took her arm and steered her out of his office.

The slightly roughened skin of his fingertips scraped over her forearm, sending tiny pinpricks of excitement along her nerve endings. She tried to ignore the sensation.

"Aggie, if anyone wants me, I'll be measuring the bulbs," he said.

"Whatever," Aggie mumbled, not even looking up from the computer printout she was studying.

"Give me the background on your first candidate," Max instructed.

"Well . . ." Kiley tried to marshal her thoughts as she followed him down the hallway, surprised he would make his decision while busy with something else. Obviously, as the head of an expanding department store chain, he didn't waste time.

"Don't bother with a whitewash job. Just stick to the facts."

"Facts can be made to prove anything you want them to," Kiley protested. "I simply want you to appreciate these kids."

"If you can't even bring yourself to name them, there's not much chance of that happening, is there?" Max said dryly.

"All right." Kiley took a deep breath, trying to adopt a businesslike manner. The problem was she was too aware of Max as a man rather than an employer. The memory of the kiss they'd shared kept getting in the way of their professional relationship.

"My first choice is Chris Prather. He's had math through the first year of calculus. More importantly from your perspective is the fact that he's a very talented artist. His eventual goal is to be able to support himself from his wildlife paintings but he knows it'll take years before he reaches that point. His parents are willing and able to support him in the meantime, but he wants the independence earning his own living would give him."

"He sounds a lot more sensible than I would have expected from someone associated with you." Max's grin robbed the words of any sting, and she smiled. "Why is a kid who's had calculus in one of your classes?"

Kiley sighed. "I mentioned him before. He's dyslexic. No matter how hard he tries, his mind won't retain words in his memory. It's as if your computer couldn't save anything, so that every time you wanted to work on something, you had to put all the information into the computer again."

"Sounds frustrating as hell."

"It is, but with the help of some dedicated teachers through the years he's learned to compensate."

"How does he compensate for not being able to read?" Max asked skeptically. Chris seemed a prime example of Kiley's overly optimistic opinion of her students' abilities.

"A reader records his textbooks on tape and Chris listens to the tapes the way another student would read a book. In fact, he's graduating in the upper five percent of his class. He could go on to college if he wanted to, but he doesn't. He already takes private art lessons twice a week at the Art Institute. Chris feels that college would take up too much of his time. I think he'll be a real asset for your store."

"It certainly sounds like it. He's not at all what I thought you had in mind. In fact, since his basic problem is a physical deficiency, I'm not so sure he wouldn't be covered under the Equal Opportunities Act," Max said thoughtfully. "I'll have Tom check it out. Once he's on board he can show some of his paintings to the manager of our home accessories department. Sam sells the work of several local artists." Max stopped in front of an office, and entered after a perfunctory knock.

"That's great." Kiley felt her spirits lift at the speed with which Max had accepted Chris. Not only accepted, but elaborated on her basic plan.

"Hi, George." Max greeted a rumpled-looking man of about fifty who was reading something at his desk. "I need to measure your plant."

"Um." George waved in the general direction of the window, where a white plastic pot with a long, gangly shoot growing out of it was sitting.

Max pulled the tape measure out of his pants pocket, carefully measured the height of the spike then jotted a number in his notebook.

"Thanks, George." Max motioned the curious Kiley from the room. One thing was certain, Max couldn't be that bad to work for, because his executives certainly weren't afraid of him. George hadn't even stopped reading.

"Now, who's next on your list?" Max asked.

"Tami Heramb. She reads at the eighth grade level, although at the start of the school year she was barely at second grade level. She's highly motivated to succeed."

"Why?"

"For her daughter's sake," Kiley said bluntly. "Tami trusted the wrong information and wound up pregnant at seventeen. The state's been footing the bills up until now, but Tami's determined that her daughter is not going to be raised on welfare like she was. A job here would be perfect for her, since you have an in-house day-care center for your employees. And because she needs a job that provides day care she'd be a loyal employee."

"What about the child's father?"

"He quit school and headed to California when Tami told him she was pregnant."

"Not an atypical reaction for a kid that age." Max grimaced. "Why on earth doesn't that precious school of yours teach them about birth control?"

"It would take days to explain why not. Besides, poor Tami thought she was practicing birth control. In common with a lot of other teenagers, she believed that you couldn't get pregnant if you made love standing up."

"You can't get pregnant if you make love standing up!" Max repeated in disbelief.

"Personally, I prefer a more comfortable position," a rotund little man said from the open doorway of the office to their left.

Kiley clenched her teeth in embarrassment and stared at the knot of Max's silver and navy striped tie. She could feel a flush staining her cheeks and she wanted nothing so much as to disappear.

"Don't be fatuous, Bill," Max said repressively. "We were discussing birth control."

"It sounds more like a game of Russian roulette to me." Bill chuckled. "If I were you, I'd visit the book department. They have several good books on the subject."

"Bill!" Max gritted out.

"Sorry. I was just trying to be helpful." The older man gave them a cherubic grin and disappeared inside his office.

"Sorry about that, Kiley, but consider Tami hired." Max knocked on the closed door beside Bill's then stuck his head inside.

"Amy, I'm here to measure your bulb. This is Kiley Sheridan."

"It doesn't need measuring. It needs a good stiff shot of fertilizer or whatever it is one feeds plants. The poor thing looks worse than I did when I had the flu last week. Hi, Kiley." Amy nodded at her.

Kiley smiled, watching as Max measured the yellowish-looking stalk on the table in the corner.

"Thanks, Amy. See you next week." Max scribbled something in his notebook, muttered, "Come on Kiley," and left. "What about the next kid on your list?" He leaned against the wall in the hallway and began jotting something in his notebook.

"Amad Varia. He comes from a large family and his father took off for parts unknown years ago. His mother works two jobs to support the kids and is almost never home. And since there was no one there to make sure Amad did his schoolwork, he didn't. It wasn't until a few months ago, when he realized he was liable to be stuck in the same kind of dead-end jobs as his mother, that he started to study."

"Hmm." Max stared blankly at the opposite wall for a few seconds then said, "Okay, add Amad. Who else is there?"

"Bubba Seaton. He's been on the school's track team for the past four years and he's bright enough, but his motivation stops at doing exactly what's necessary to stay eligible for track and cross country."

"Oh, great. An employee who does the least he can get away with."

"That's not what I said. I said he does what's necessary to achieve his goal. Who knows, he could decide he wants your job!" she said tartly.

"Point taken." Max entered an empty office and quickly measured a thick bushy plant that had buds forming.

"Would you mind telling me what you're doing?" Her curiosity finally got the better of her.

"I'm checking on how amaryllis bulbs grow under varying light and heat conditions."

"Why?"

"Because we're going to include prepackaged amaryllis bulbs as part of our Christmas stock, but the directions for them list ideal conditions. Few of our customers will have ideal conditions. I want to grow them here so we can write a tip sheet for our customers."

"Very thorough," she said approvingly.

"We have to be. Retailing is a highly competitive field and you have to try to gain every advantage you can. Now, what about the next person on your list?"

"Wayland Riveras. He has a big advantage over most of the kids in my classes. He has an intact nuclear family. Unfortunately, it's a family that's moved a lot. Wayland has been to ten different schools in his life and some of them have been less than ideal. He follows a pretty typical pattern. With every move he fell a little farther behind, until today he's reading six years below grade level. But on the positive side, he's never missed a day of school, and I'd match his sense of integrity against anyone's."

"All right, include Wayland."

"You won't be sorry," she said with perfect sincerity. "The last person is Dawn Reid. She's been in and out of foster homes for years, but they've always been short stays." Kiley sighed. "Usually just long enough to mess up any progress she might have been making in school. You see, her mother is a diabetic. The doctors can't seem to convince her that she has to be extremely careful about her diet. To say nothing of the necessity of taking her insulin shots on a regular basis. Mrs. Reid'll go for months being careful, and then, probably because she feels so good, she'll indulge in something like a box of chocolates and wind up right back in the hospital while they try to stabilize her."

"It sounds like a variation of a game some alcoholics play about it being safe to take just one little drink."

Kiley grimaced. "Well, if it is, it's a deadly game. The result of all this is that there's a lot of stress in Dawn's life and like most teenagers she hasn't learned to cope with it very effectively."

"Take my word for it, age doesn't help anyone in trying to cope with a parent who persists in indulging in self-destructive behavior. My father died a lingering, excruciatingly painful death from lung cancer despite the fact that my mother and I had been begging him to quit smoking for over twenty years." Max's face tightened under the force of his dark memories, and Kiley shivered at the bleak expression in his eyes.

"So we add Dawn to your list and you help her learn coping techniques. And speaking of your classes, I thought you might hold them in one of our conference rooms."

Max opened a door and gestured her inside. The room was small but luxurious enough to enhance her students' fragile sense of self-worth, Kiley noted with pleasure. A thick beige carpet covered the floor, complementing the mahogany paneling. There were no windows, but several colorful oil paintings on the walls added visual interest.

"It's great," she enthused. "It looks so much more professional than a traditional classroom would. Thanks, Max."

"You're welcome." His eyes gleamed at her obvious pleasure. "Ask Aggie about any supplies you want, and if she's not around you can ask Tom."

"Yes, Tom." Her spirits plummeted at the thought of the head of personnel.

"He isn't as bad as you think," Max insisted.

"He couldn't be as bad as I think," Kiley said dryly. "Not and still be running around loose. If it's all the same to you, I'd just as soon keep all contact with him to an absolute minimum."

"It isn't all the same to me. I expect all my employees to maintain a professional demeanor toward each other no matter what their personal feelings."

"I'm not your employee," she grumbled.

"You're going to be the role model for six of them," he shot back. "Besides, think a minute, Kiley. You can't just ignore Tom. He's essential to the eventual absorption of your students into the store. Ask yourself why you dislike Tom so much."

"That's easy. Because he refused to hire my students. Every argument I advanced was met with some smugly middle-class platitude."

"Any why do you suppose that was?"

"Because Tom Preston is smugly middle-class?"

"I'm serious," Max insisted.

Kiley threw up her hands in defeat. "All right. I suppose if I was objective about this I'd concede that Tom was simply trying to protect the store from my students, whom he sees as undesirable employees. He just doesn't want them around. Kind of like my principal."

"And yet you manage to function quite well at school despite Mr. Beamish," Max pointed out.

"Hmm." Kiley frowned thoughtfully. "I guess if I'm going to be absolutely honest, the truth is that I've made Tom the focus of my frustration over not being able to find the kids jobs, and that really isn't fair."

"Or productive," Max added.

"No," she agreed. "Well, I may not know what constitutes professional behavior in the business world but I certainly know what it is in teaching. I'll treat Tom as I would a new principal who's showing signs of hostility."

"Good." He gave her a warm, approving smile that sent a surge of pleasure through her. "You can make a start at forming some kind of viable relationship with him Sunday at the picnic."

She frowned, remembering that a picnic had been mentioned before. "What picnic?"

"The store kicks off the summer season with a picnic for the employees and their families at my home. It's the one Sunday a year the stores are closed."

"It must be an awful lot of work."

"Not really. We have an outside firm cater it. In fact I think it'd be a good idea for you to bring your students along, too. It'll be a chance for them to meet everyone in relaxed surroundings."

"That sounds like a great idea," she said. "Then if there's nothing else..." she said, having too much pride to allow him to think that she was angling for his company now that their business was concluded.

"Yes."

"Yes?" She looked at him in confusion.

"Yes, there's something else," he elaborated. "You were helping me measure the amaryllis spikes, remember?"

"Wrong. You were measuring the spikes. I was simply watching in amazement that you hadn't delegated the job to someone else."

"Haven't you ever heard the old saying that if you want something done right, do it yourself?"

"I've heard a lot of old sayings in my life," she said dryly. "And I've got better sense than to believe them all."

"Bah! That's the trouble with the world today. There's no faith."

"Certainly not much blind faith, and I for one think it's a great idea. People ought to think instead of simply reacting."

"And do you always think before you react?" Max eyed her speculatively.

"I try," she said repressively, not trusting the gleam of devilment in his eye.

"You certainly do." He stopped in front of a closed door and knocked. When no one answered, he knocked again then went in.

"Ha! She's gone."

"It would appear so." Kiley glanced around the empty office. "Although I don't know about she. From the looks of these plants, this office should belong to the Jolly Green Giant. They're fantastic!" Kiley touched the lush foliage of a monstrous Boston fern. "And look at that amaryllis." Kiley's eye was caught by the blaze of red to the right of the room's one window. "Her plant appears to be weeks ahead of the others."

"It shouldn't be. The lighting isn't much better than the last office we were in." Max opened the door to what appeared to be a closet and stepped inside.

"Don't tell me you put a bulb in there?" Kiley followed him in.

"Of course not." Max began to rummage through the contents of the overloaded shelves.

"Then what are you looking for?" She automatically took the box he handed her and set it on the floor.

"A grow light," he muttered. "I know she's giving that thing shots with a grow light the minute my back's turned."

"No! Surely not. Why, the duplicity of it positively boggles the mind." Kiley giggled at his aggrieved expression.

"It isn't funny," he insisted. "She's messing up my test results."

"I can see the headlines now. Steroid scandal in the plant world. Illicit exposure to grow light skews tests results." She began to laugh uproariously.

"You have a skewed sense of humor." Max reached out and pulled her against him. Kiley could feel his hard body pressing into her soft curves from breast to thigh, and the sensation was electrifying.

Her eyes widened, and her laughter died in her throat. Her gaze was caught and held by the reflected light dancing in his eyes. Her eyes dropped lower to trace his firm lips and heat began to build in her chest at the memory of the feel and taste of them.

"You smell wonderful." Max's warm breath wafted over her cheek, causing the skin to tighten. His hand cupped the back of her head, holding it steady as he brushed his lips across hers. "And you taste even better."

"Max?" His name came out on a sigh of longing, mingling her warm breath with his. She reached up and stroked her hand across his cheek. The rasped silk texture of his skin against her palm sent pinpricks of awareness skittering along her nerve endings. Kiley's lips parted invitingly, and his arms tightened, binding her unresisting body yet closer to him. His mouth covered hers with a hungry intensity he made no effort to hide.

"Go use your own office!" An annoyed female voice poured over Kiley's sensitized nerves like a douse of cold water, and she instinctively tried to close the sound out.

Max lifted his head and turned to glare at the petite woman in the doorway.

"Max!"

Kiley watched as the woman's mouth opened in shock.

Strangely enough, the woman's amazement made Kiley feel much better. Obviously, Max was not in the habit of being caught in compromising situations or this woman wouldn't have been so surprised when she recognized him.

"We were looking for a grow light," Max said.

"Bad idea." The woman gave him an innocent smile, which sat oddly with the mischief in her hazel eyes. "If what appears to be between you two grows anymore, it isn't going to be suitable for a family store."

Although embarrassed, Kiley forced herself to meet the woman's eyes. She refused to demean that kiss with an apology. Something that shattering should be celebrated as the uniquely satisfying experience it was.

Stepping out of the protective shelter of Max's arms, she said, "Actually Max was simply demonstrating some of the finer points of his customer appreciation techniques."

With a wicked smile at the surprised woman, Kiley bolted out the door.

# 5

AT NINE-THIRTY on a Sunday morning, Kiley pulled her van into the parking lot behind the downtown Winthrops. She had no trouble locating the yellow car that Chris had said his mother would let him use to pick up the other students. As Kiley stopped beside the car, four of her students spilled out and hurried toward her.

"Hi, Miss Sheridan." Wayland pulled open the van's sliding door and clambered into the back seat. "Those two buses arrived a few minutes ago." He gestured to his right.

"There was only a couple of people waiting to get on." Dawn climbed into the front passenger seat.

"That's because they aren't scheduled to leave for over an hour yet," Kiley explained. "If you want, you can ride in the buses with the other employees. You're just as much invited guests as they are."

Four pairs of horrified eyes turned in her direction.

"It's bad enough going somewhere you've never been with friends, but in a bus full of strangers—" Chris shuddered.

"This way we'll get there first and we can watch them arrive," Dawn said.

"Yeah," Tami echoed. "Here, Miss Sheridan, would you hold Jenny while I strap her car seat in?"

"With pleasure." Kiley reached across the seat and took the small, warm bundle out of Tami's arms, smiling at the baby's round little face. "What a sweetie you are," Kiley crooned, dropping a kiss on her wispy hair. "And you smell so good. Just like baby powder. I love the way babies smell."

"That's cause you don't know how much work it is to keep them smelling like that." Tami gave Kiley a look that seemed to reverse their ages. "Not but what it ain't worth it," she added, taking the baby and buckling her into her seat.

"Hi, Miss Sheridan." Amad shoved his gym bag under the middle seat and climbed into the rear with Chris and Wayland. "Didn't you guys bring swimsuits along? That lady down at the office where we filled out all them forms on Friday said there'd be swimming at the picnic."

"Thanks, Amad. I forgot to get our bags out of the trunk." Chris scrambled out and ran to his car.

Dawn groaned. "Don't mention them forms. I never saw such a nebby bunch of people in my life. They were even worse than that social worker that kept coming around when Mom was in the hospital last winter."

"Weren't they just," Tami said with a sigh. "But at least it's all done, and tomorrow Jenny and I start at Winthrops."

"What's she going to do? Give screaming lessons?" Amad chortled.

Tami glared at him. "Jenny doesn't scream. She's a very good baby."

"Sure she is." Amad grinned. "Why, I must have heard you say so at least twenty times a day. You're—"

"Has anyone seen Bubba?" Kiley broke off the squabble with the ease of long practice.

"Oh, yeah. I meant to tell you, Miss Sheridan. Bubba called right before Chris picked me up," Wayland said. "He tried to call you but you'd already left. He said he was sorry, but that something had come up and he couldn't come."

"I hope nothing's happened at home," Kiley said slowly. He'd seemed excited about coming when she'd seen him on Friday.

"I don't think so," Wayland said. "He sounded all excited, kinda like it was his birthday or somethin'. But when I asked what was happening, he just said he didn't want to talk about it for fear of jinxing the deal."

"Well, in that case, since we're all here, we'd best be off. Is everyone buckled in?" Kiley asked.

"Me and Jenny's safe," Tami said.

"Me, too." Dawn gestured toward her shoulder strap.

"Same here," Chris called.

"Yo," Amad added.

Kiley waited a second then looked over her shoulder.

"Wayland?"

"Ah, seat belts is dumb," Wayland objected. "And, besides, supposing the car smashes and burst into flames and I turn into a charcoal briquette because I was trapped by my seat belt."

"That's a highly unlikely scenario." Kiley gave him a level stare.

"But it could happen," Wayland insisted.

"The subject is not open for discussion," Kiley stated firmly. "If you wish to ride in my car, you'll wear a seat belt."

"But—" Wayland sputtered.

"If you won't, there's the bus." She nodded toward the window. "Feel free to use it."

"Aw." Wayland's voice dropped to a grumble, but he buckled the seat belt.

"We're off." Kiley turned the van around and headed into the street. "Remember, if you want to come back before I do, those buses return here every half hour."

"Why?" Dawn asked.

"So people can leave the picnic whenever they wish," Kiley said.

"No, I mean, why use buses? Why don't people just drive out like we're doing?" Dawn said.

"Because there isn't enough parking at Mr. Winthrop's home. By using buses, people can leave their cars in the store parking lot."

"So why is he letting you bring a car?" Tami demanded.

"Out of the goodness of his heart?" Kiley suggested.

"You wanta watch it, Miss Sheridan. Men don't do nothin' out of the goodness of their heart. Their thoughts are usually centered a little lower," Tami whispered across the front seat.

"I'll remember that." Kiley was touched at Tami's concern even while she deplored the circumstances that had given the younger girl such a jaundiced view of men.

The traffic on the road to McLean was light, and they made good time. Kiley had no trouble finding the turnoff, and ten minutes later she swung the car into Max's driveway.

"Holy shit!" Amad whistled as he caught sight of the house. "Um, sorry, Miss Sheridan. I meant holy, um... Never mind. But will you look at that place!"

"Wow!" Dawn craned her head out the window for a better look. "I ain't never seen nothing like that outside the movies."

"Get your head in the car," Kiley ordered.

"I'm going to have me a house like that someday," Amad vowed. "Just you wait and see."

"Not me," Tami said. "It's too big. You'd never be finished cleaning it."

"If you can afford to buy it, you can afford a cleaning woman to do it for you," Wayland said practically.

"And who wants some stranger poking into your things," Tami scoffed. "Not me and Jenny. We're gonna have us a nice little two-bedroom town house in a few years."

"Hey, look at all those tents." Chris pointed to the grassy, rolling meadow behind the garages as Kiley followed the driveway to the back of the house. "It looks like something out of King Arthur and Camelot."

"Naw." Wayland hurriedly unbuckled his seat belt as Kiley parked the car. "It looks like a carnival to me."

"It looks like fun," Dawn said enthusiastically. "They've even got a merry-go-round for the kids set up. They—" Dawn's voice trailed away as she caught sight of Max walking toward them.

"Geez," Amad muttered. "It's him. What's he want?"

"He's our host, Amad." Kiley hoped the pleasure she felt at the sight of Max wasn't apparent in her face.

"So?" Amad asked.

"A host always greets his guests. Out you go."

Her students piled out of the car and stood awkwardly as Max approached.

Max shot Kiley a penetrating gaze then turned to her students. "Good morning," Max greeted them. "You're just in time. Daniel was looking for some men to help him carry the equipment for the games out to the playing field. So if you'd care to volunteer before he sees you and drafts you . . ."

"Sure," Chris said. "We'd be glad to help."

"Yeah," Amad agreed. "If we can put our bags somewhere."

"You can leave them in the house," Max said. "I'll show you. If you two girls, no, three—" Max smiled at the baby "—want to come along . . ."

"No, thanks." Dawn stepped back and gave him a nervous smile. "I think I'll just go sit down and watch things a while." She gestured toward one of the lawn chairs, which had been set up under the trees.

"Me and Jenny'll go with her," Tami said. "Fresh air's good for Jenny, and this here's fresher'n what we got in D.C. It don't smell like nothing but flowers. See you later, Miss Sheridan." Tami, with the nervous Dawn beside her, headed for the shade of a large oak tree while Max led the rest of the group through a pair of French doors and into a small sitting room.

"Holy s—" Amad smothered the expression in a cough.

Kiley followed his rapt gaze, seeing the massive silver tea service on the mahogany breakfront just inside the door.

Amad picked up a creamer, tested the weight of it in his hand and said, "How much is something like this worth?"

"It's Georgian, isn't it?" Kiley tried to smooth over the awkward silence that fell at Amad's question.

"Yes," Max replied, still watching Amad. He frowned as the boy put the piece down with fingerprints all over its gleaming surface.

Max's expression infuriated Kiley. It was hardly Amad's fault that he lacked social graces. Anymore than it was to Max's credit that he had them. That had been decided by the accident of their births. What was important was how Amad learned from the opportunity he was being given.

"One of my relatives brought it back with him when he returned from a trip to England in the seventeen hundreds," Max elaborated.

"It must be nice. All my relatives ever bring back is towels from motels. So where can I dump this?" Amad gestured with his bag.

"Just put it anywhere," Max said, and Amad did, dropping it at his feet and pushing it against the wall. The other two boys followed suit.

"See ya later," Amad said, and accompanied by Chris and Wayland hurried out to look for Daniel.

"What's the matter?" Kiley asked as Max watched the boys cross the lawn.

"Nothing." Max turned toward her.

"Nothing doesn't make you frown," she persisted.

"It's nothing I can put my finger on," he said slowly. "It was just the look on that kid's face when he was manhandling the silver."

"The kid's name is Amad, and he was probably coveting it, the same as me. The only difference between us is that at my age I'm better able to disguise my greed."

"Maybe." Max didn't sound convinced and Kiley had to bite her lip to keep from protesting. Mainly because she wasn't exactly sure what she was protesting. Surely Max couldn't have decided Amad was untrustworthy

simply because he liked what was, after all, an exquisite piece of silver? Searching for a safe, neutral subject, she asked, "How long has the store held this picnic
for its employees?"

"Since eighteen thirty-nine. Although nowadays
we're really too big to hold it out here."

"Then why not move it to one of the area's parks?"

"What! And mess with tradition? When I was a kid
I used to pretend those tents belonged to Genghis Khan
and that I was defending the house against his hordes.
And my grandfather told me that when he was a boy
he used to pretend he was fighting off the Indians.
Surely my son should have the chance to defend the
house against invaders, too."

"Today's invaders come from space," Kiley murmured as an image of a younger, softer Max formed in
her mind. Would his son have his dark hair and brilliant blue eyes, or would he look like his mother? The
image shifted, reforming itself with brown hair and
chocolate-brown eyes.

No. She firmly banished the strangely tantalizing
picture. Max's mythical children had nothing to do with
her.

"They don't come from space. They come from the
fevered imaginings of some toy company," Max said in
disgust.

Kiley shuddered. "I've noticed a few of their recent
offerings. Whatever happened to dolls and toy trains?"

"Fashion dolls are perennial best-sellers."

"Not that kind of doll. The cuddly kind that says mama."

"She now has a cassette player that spits out phrases in six languages. It's a big seller among the yuppie crowd. But the buying public isn't our worry today. While we've got the time, let's see what's going wrong with the catering." Max started toward the door.

"What could go wrong?" She fell into step beside him.

"The possibilities defy the imagination. In fact, the reality sometimes defies the imagination. Last year one of the waiters managed to get drunk and decided to go for a swim in the pool." He opened the kitchen door and motioned her through.

"Annoying, but essentially harmless." Kiley carefully threaded her way through the crowd of people working there.

"Not when you consider the fact that he stripped first." Max shook his head mournfully. "I hadn't realized that I had that many straitlaced people working for me."

"Really?" Kiley frowned, trying to imagine the scene. She couldn't. "Ah, well, this all looks pretty efficient." She smiled at a large man chopping vegetables with a huge knife.

He glared at her.

"Yes, everything does seem to be under control in here." Max started toward the door, and Kiley, after one last cautious look at the man with the knife, followed him.

"In here, Max," his mother called from the sitting room as they passed the door. "Good afternoon, my dear," she greeted Kiley. "I saw you from my bedroom window as you drove around the house. I hope you'll introduce me to your students later."

"Certainly." Kiley smiled warmly at her. "At the moment the boys are helping set things up and Dawn and Tami are getting some fresh air and entertaining the baby."

"Coming early was a good idea," Mrs. Winthrop approved. "It'll give your students a chance to feel at ease before everyone else arrives."

"It was a good idea, but I can't take credit for it," she said fairly. "It was Max's idea."

"Speaking of good ideas, would you like something cold to drink, Kiley?"

"Yes, please."

Max extracted two cans from the tiny refrigerator hidden in the mahogany breakfront, opened them and handed one to her.

Kiley wrapped her hot fingers around the icy can, letting the chill seep into her body.

"How's the caterer doing?" Mrs. Winthrop asked. "I stuck my head in the kitchen about an hour ago and was told quite firmly that my presence was not required."

"Efficiently. I hope this year we won't have a drunken waiter skinny-dipping in the pool," Max said.

His mother agreed. "But you must admit it added a certain something to the day."

"An X rating," Max said dryly. "The only good thing about it was that it happened during the magic show and the kids were all well away from the action. I just hope this year's affair manages to go off without any disasters."

"Nonsense." Kiley laughed. "Things like the waiter are what make an event memorable. People will still be talking about it years from now. Probably because most people would love to do something so unconventional but don't have the nerve."

"Does that mean you're a closet skinny-dipper?" Max's eyes gleamed with sudden interest.

"It's very enjoyable," his mother unexpectedly added. "Provided of course that you do it with the right person."

"Mother!"

"And they said my generation was the prudish one," she said tartly. "And speaking of my generation, that Greek man called."

"I am not a prude, and what Greek?"

"Stavros. The one who always tries to flirt with me. He called while you were outside and said it was important that he talk to you as soon as you came in. I left his number in your study."

"I wonder what . . ." Max ran his fingers through his hair, creating an endearingly disheveled look that made Kiley long to brush back a strand.

"I'd better call him and find out what's wrong. Kiley. . ." Max turned to her.

"Don't worry about me. I'll just wander around and look at things."

"Why don't you keep me company instead," Mrs. Winthrop suggested. "I was about to take my daily constitutional and you're sensibly dressed."

Kiley shot her a quick glance, wondering if Mrs. Winthrop was being critical. She hadn't been too sure what to wear to the picnic, but she'd finally decided that while it might be at the home of a millionaire, the majority of the guests would be middle class, so she'd dressed accordingly, choosing a colorful lemon cotton top with white shorts and white jogging shoes.

The look of honest appraisal in Mrs. Winthrop's eyes reassured Kiley and she forced herself to smile and accept the offer even though she would have preferred to stay close to Max and her students. But Max had things to do, and her students wouldn't thank her for watching over them like a mother hen.

"Kiley." Max gave her a worried frown. "You don't have to . . ."

"And I didn't have to invite her," Mrs. Winthrop said mildly. "I did so because I like her."

"If you're sure, Kiley?" he persisted.

"Sure I'm sure," she said, wondering why Max was concerned. Did he think she was going to push his mother too hard? She certainly had better sense than to maintain a pace that would exhaust an elderly lady.

Forty minutes later, Kiley was no longer the least bit concerned with the state of Mrs. Winthrop's health. She was too worried about her own.

She trailed Mrs. Winthrop to the house in a state of acute exhaustion. Her breath was coming in short gasps and her legs ached abominably.

"Are you all right, dear?" Mrs. Winthrop shooed her through the front door.

Kiley staggered into the cool house, pinned an artificial smile on her face and lied, "Certainly. A good workout always makes me feel better." She was not going to admit that she'd just been walked into the ground by a senior citizen.

"My sentiments exactly." Mrs. Winthrop beamed at her. "Why don't you go see if Max has finished with his phone call while I change for the picnic."

"Sure," Kiley said, having no intention of looking for Max. She had more pride than that. Besides, she thought ruefully, even if she found him, she wouldn't be able to do more than gasp at him like a stranded fish.

After Mrs. Winthrop had disappeared up the stairs Kiley limped into the library. She winced as she caught sight of herself in the antique mirror above the fireplace. Her face was bright red and her hair was clinging to her hot cheeks.

Wearily, she sank down into one of the brown leather chairs beside the fireplace and propped her aching feet on a matching ottoman. Leaning her head back, she closed her eyes and concentrated on getting her breathing under control. Next week she was definitely going to join a health club and get in shape, she vowed.

"Damn!"

Kiley jumped at the sound of Max's roughly bitten off expletive.

"I should never have let you go with her."

"Not without an explicit warning." She chuckled weakly. "Your mother would make Jack LaLaine proud. She—" Kiley gasped as an agonizing cramp seized her calf.

She grabbed her calf, but Max pushed her hands away. Kneeling beside her, he grasped the constricted muscle and began to knead it.

"Don't!" Kiley jerked as waves of pain radiated up her leg.

"It's the only way." Max's voice deepened at her obvious distress.

"Wrong, I could commit hara-kiri," she gritted.

"On a blue Oriental carpet?" His voice was threaded with laughter. "I'd never get the stains out."

"Thanks, it's nice to know where I stand. Agh," she moaned.

"You aren't capable of standing anywhere. What kind of cool down did you have?"

"I stood under the air-conditioning vent." She stifled a gasp as the pressure his fingers were exerting deepened.

"Do you mean to tell me that you walked three miles in thirty-five minutes and never bothered to gradually cool down?" Max stared at her in disbelief.

"There's nothing gradual about your mother. She takes off with all the enthusiasm of Sherman marching on Atlanta. And how do you know it was thirty-five minutes? It felt more like hours."

"Because my mother always walks three miles in thirty-five minutes. Quit squirming around."

"I'm in pain!" she wailed. "I need sympathy, not abuse."

"You need to have your head examined for not telling my mother you couldn't keep up."

"How could I tell a woman her age I couldn't stand the pace?" she muttered.

"Try opening your mouth. You never seem to have any trouble doing so when I'm around," he said dryly. "Next time—"

"Next time I'll know better," she said, wondering if he was speaking generally or if he intended to invite her again. The idea excited her and yet made her vaguely nervous. She was much too attracted to Max. She was supposed to convert him to her way of thinking about her students, and a one-sided emotional fixation on her part was not going to make the job any easier. She was going to have to put a stop to her growing feelings or they could cloud her judgment and obscure her purpose.

"Just relax." Max's voice deepened, soothing her jumbled thoughts. The intense cramp was fading, and she was becoming much more aware of other things. Such as his touch. And the feeling of his strong fingers pressing into her skin. A burning warmth seemed to flow from his fingertips into her flesh, unlocking her tortured muscles. From there, the heat spread upward to tighten around her chest, constricting her breathing.

Kiley studied Max from beneath half-closed lids. His expression was intent, as if what he was doing was the most important thing in the world. As if she was the most important thing in the world. It was an intoxicating thought.

"Any better?" Max gave her a quick glance.

"A little," she said slowly, reluctant to end the exquisitely pleasurable sensation.

"Is this a case of kiss and make it better?" Max asked huskily.

Kiley's gaze met his and became ensnared by the hot glow burning in his eyes. Max was as caught up in the sensual excitement burning between them as she was. The knowledge fed her sense of self-confidence, and she put her hands on his shoulders. The muscles bunched beneath her fingertips, and she shuddered at the power of his body.

"You have to be the most inept exerciser I've seen in a long time." The warm tenderness in his voice caressed her, and Kiley responded to it, lifting her head invitingly.

He lowered his head until his lips hovered a tantalizing fraction of an inch from hers. She could almost taste the coffee that flavored his breath.

"Max?" Her voice was a plea, and he responded by closing the gap between them. She shivered at the pressure of his firm lips and threaded her fingers through his hair, reveling in its silken texture.

Max's mouth left hers and his lips wandered caressingly across her cheekbone to nuzzle the sensitive skin behind her ear.

Kiley trembled beneath the onslaught of sensation, wanting more, much more than this.

It was almost a relief when his hand slipped beneath her cotton top to find and cup her small bare breast. Blindly, she twisted her head, seeking the taste of his mouth. The roar of a large vehicle turning into the driveway shattered her absorption and she pulled away, disoriented.

Max's roughly bitten off expletive exactly expressed how she felt. She wanted to consign everyone, from Max's thoroughly likable mother to her students, to perdition. She wanted to seal herself away with Max in a place where they could be alone. In a place where she could concentrate on nothing but Max and how he made her feel.

Max grimaced as he dropped a quick kiss on the tip of her nose. "You look like someone just stole your dessert and I feel like . . ." Someone just snatched away my whole meal, he thought ruefully, not fully understanding what had happened. A lighthearted kiss had quickly escalated out of control and he'd forgotten such mundane considerations as the fact that they were in a room with the door open and the house full of people. He was fast coming to realize that there was no such thing as sharing a casual kiss with Kiley.

He reached down and pulled her to her feet. "Our guests are arriving. Let's go welcome them."

Our guests? She pondered his choice of words as she accompanied him to the front door. Surely the *our* referred to his mother and him? She dared to hope that wasn't what Max had meant.

The sight of Tom Preston drove the question from her mind. Cautiously, she studied Tom as she walked down the front steps beside Max, trying to decide whether she should make a start on forging the beginnings of some kind of working relationship with him today, when the relatively relaxed atmosphere of the picnic should make the task easier, or wait until they were working together in the store.

"Hi, there. How are things growing?" A cheerful voice greeted her and Kiley turned, groaning inwardly when she recognized the woman who'd discovered her and Max in the closet.

"I'm working on a bumper crop of chagrin and embarrassment," Kiley said ruefully. "By the way, my name is Kiley Sheridan."

"You can't possibly think that's news, can you?" The woman laughed. "The whole store knows all about you."

"All?" Kiley winced.

"I may listen to gossip, but I don't embellish on it. Besides, I'm holding that particular piece of information in reserve to use if our fearless leader should get lucky and find my grow light. I'm Jane Anderson, the senior buyer for children's wear."

"I'm happy to meet you and I'm even happier to hear about your discretion. I feel exposed enough without them knowing—"

"What? That you're normal?" Jane scoffed. "Most of us would give our eyeteeth if Max'd even notice us, let alone snatch kisses in other people's closets."

"It isn't like that," Kiley insisted.

Jane shrugged good-naturedly. "Whatever you say. I for one am going to get something tall and cool to drink. Want to come along?"

Kiley shot a quick glance at Max. He was surrounded by people, including a preschooler who appeared to be beating Max's leg with a sucker.

"One of the senior vice presidents' kids." Jane followed her glance.

"There's so many of them," Kiley said, despairing of ever figuring out who all these people were, let alone forming working relationships with them.

"Naw, the brat's an only, for which the world should give thanks. He's spoiled rotten."

"No, I meant so many people work at the store."

"Well, we do have eight stores in the area and almost everyone brought their families with them. Come on. I'll introduce you around."

"Thanks." Kiley forced herself to go with the friendly Jane, missing the narrow-eyed glance Max gave her as she moved away.

Kiley spent the next half hour being introduced to a bewildering array of people, the vast majority of whom proved quite friendly, if a little too curious about her relationship with Max for her peace of mind.

She was standing beside the Olympic-size pool politely listening to Cora Someone-or-other relating exactly how she'd managed to convince the buying public that it really wanted the new high-cut swimsuits when she felt the hair on the back of her neck prickle warningly. As if she'd suddenly entered an electrical force field, she thought fancifully, then jumped when she felt the warmth of a man's slightly roughened fingertips close around her upper arm. A surge of awareness poured through her, and she took a deep breath, inhaling the lingering scent of a man's cologne. She didn't have to turn to know who it was. She'd recognize Max's touch anywhere.

"Hi, Max," Cora greeted him cheerfully. "Great picnic you've got here."

"Thanks," Max smiled at her. "If you'll excuse us, I want to borrow Kiley."

"Sure." Cora waved them away then looked around for a fresh victim to regale with her latest coup.

"Say thank you, Max."

"Thank you, Max," Kiley said in heartfelt tones. "Cora seems nice, but I was slowly sinking under the blow-by-blow description of the latest in swimwear marketing. If she should ever find out that I'm still using the same suit I bought when I was in college . . ." Kiley shuddered.

He grinned at her. "My silence can be bought."

"I'm morally opposed to blackmail," she said primly.

"I think you'd like my price," he added persuasively, his eyes focused on her lips with an intensity that made her shiver.

# 6

KILEY SMILED as she watched Tami holding Jenny so the baby could splash in the huge portable wading pool, which had been set up under the shade of a centuries-old oak tree. Turning, she searched the mass of bodies in the inground pool, looking for the boys.

"Contemplating going for a swim?"

Kiley jumped as Max seemed to suddenly materialize beside her.

"You startled me," she gasped. "I didn't realize you were around."

"I brought you one of these tarts to try before they're all gone." He handed her a small pastry, topped with an oversize strawberry and covered with a glistening red glaze.

"Thanks." Kiley took a bite, her eyes widening in surprise as a citrus taste flooded her mouth. She swallowed and peered closer at the tart, noticing the thin yellow layer beneath the strawberry. "There's lemon in this. It's delicious." She finished the treat in two bites then nodded toward the pool. "Tell me, who's that young man beside Amad?"

Max followed her gaze. "The blonde?"

"Uh-huh."

"David Mallings. He's a new college graduate we hired a few weeks ago for our management training program."

"He certainly seems to know everyone already." Kiley watched as he said something to a young woman sitting on the edge of the pool. She splashed water at him and flounced off while David and Amad laughed uproariously.

"He should. He's been coming to these picnics since he was born. Jim, his dad, is one of our senior vice presidents."

"I see," Kiley said slowly, still watching David's and Amad's horseplay.

"What's wrong?" Max asked. "They look like they're having fun."

"Nothing's wrong." Kiley determinedly shook off the faint feeling of unease she had that someone with David's background and four years older would make a friend of Amad. David probably simply liked him, she reassured herself.

"David'll be good for Amad—"

"Maybe Amad will be good for David!"

Before Max could answer, they were hailed by Tom Preston.

Reminding herself that she needed to establish a professional relationship with the man, she pasted a welcoming smile on her face. It would be easier to deal with Tom Preston this time, she encouraged herself. This time she wasn't approaching him as a suppliant.

This time she had a recognized standing in the store. As did her students.

"Miss Sheridan." He nodded at Kiley then turned to Max. "Bill mentioned you were looking for me, Max?"

"Yes, I thought you might like to talk to Kiley about her students." Max sent her a questioning look she had no trouble interpreting. He was willing to stay and lend her moral support. Her heart warmed even as she rejected his unspoken offer. She couldn't allow herself to get into the habit of using him as a crutch in dealing with Tom. Not only did she have too much pride, but Tom would never believe her students could be useful employees if their teacher needed someone to hold her hand when she was faced with unpleasant tasks.

"I'd appreciate a moment of your time, Mr. Preston," Kiley said briskly. "If you'll excuse us, Max?" She was rewarded by a gleam of approval in Max's eyes.

Tom watched Max leave then said, "You know, there's more of his father in him than I thought."

"I'm sure that would please Max," Kiley said. "He speaks of his father with a great deal of love."

"I was referring to his father's hiring practices. He—"

"Max told me about that. But surely you can't honestly believe that my six students represent a threat to your store?"

"No, but what is it they say about a foot in the door?"

"Probably the same thing they say about not going looking for trouble," she said tartly. "Listen, Mr. Preston—"

"Tom will do."

"Tom. I know you don't like me, but—"

"You're wrong there, Kiley. I don't know you well enough to like or dislike you. What I do think is that you're an impossibly naive do-gooder who carries with her the potential to cause a great deal of damage."

"I am not the least bit naive."

"About business you are," Tom insisted, "or you wouldn't feel that getting these kids jobs is going to change anything. They'll bring the same set of attitudes to the store as they brought to school. And they weren't much of a success at school, were they?"

"That's a generalization, and like most generalizations, only half-true. Chris was an outstanding student. And as for the others, they hung in there and got their high school diplomas, so the least you can say about them is that they're tenacious."

"A trait they no doubt picked up from you," Tom said dryly.

"Do you intend to play on their insecurities?" Kiley asked bluntly.

"No," Tom replied promptly. "I may not have approved of hiring them in the first place, but that decision's already been made. All that remains now is to try to lick them into some kind of shape."

"And how do you intend to do that?"

"Ah, but I thought that was your job," Tom countered.

"And you'll let me do it without interference?"

"Within reason. You may not believe this, but all I want is what's best for the store."

"What's best for the store and what's best for my students are not necessarily mutually exclusive."

"Perhaps, perhaps not. Time will tell. Harry!" Tom raised his voice to get the attention of a man about fifteen feet from them. Gesturing for the man to come over, he said to Kiley, "Max mentioned that you had a kid for Harry's department."

"Harry?"

"Layouts and displays." He turned to the man who was approaching. "Harry, I'd like you to meet Kiley Sheridan. She's going to be guiding some of our new hires through the pitfalls of retailing this summer. Kiley, this is Harry Montez."

"Hi." Kiley started to extend her hand, realized that he had a heaping plate of food in one hand and a large drink in the other, and nodded instead. Harry Montez certainly didn't look like her idea of an artist, she thought ruefully. He looked more like an oversize teddy bear.

"Ha! So you're finally going to get me a little more help," he said to Tom. "And not before time. How much experience has this new hire got?" He shot the question at Kiley.

"Well . . . none," she admitted.

"Good," was the response. "That way I won't have to spend a lot of time breaking him of bad habits."

Kiley swallowed a grin. Harry made Chris sound like a puppy he was going to take in hand. Deciding she might as well tell him the facts now as later, she said, "Chris is dyslexic."

"Hell, I don't care where he's from."

"No, I mean he has a physical handicap that makes it impossible for him to read."

"My secretary reads. My artists draw. What kind of artist is he?"

"Great!" Kiley's sincerity was unmistakable.

"No problem then." Harry nodded at her, and with a muttered goodbye wandered off toward a table.

"Tell me, how much truth is there in what you told Harry?"

"Truth?" Kiley blinked at Tom. "All of it, of course."

"I meant about the...dyslexia, I think you called it."

"It's a physical malfunction of the brain. I'll copy an article about it from one of my teaching journals," Kiley offered, knowing facts were the best way to combat prejudice. "That is, if you'll read it," she challenged him.

"Word of honor," he said with mock solemnity.

"Kiley." Max suddenly appeared beside her. "I need your leg."

"My leg?" Kiley glanced at her tanned limbs in puzzlement. "What are you planning on doing with it?"

"Win the three-legged race, of course," Max said. He grabbed her arm, and with a hasty goodbye to the grinning Tom, began to drag her toward the rolling lawns behind the house.

"I gave up races when I got too old for summer camp," Kiley said.

"You have to," Max insisted.

"That just goes to show what you know," Kiley replied succinctly.

"You do, too," he argued. "The executives have a duty to make this a pleasant time for the store's employees. Not to stand around enjoying one another's company."

"Enjoying..." Kiley sputtered. "I was trying to mend fences with that personnel manager of yours."

"He's not that bad."

"No," she admitted. "He's not the ogre I built him up to be in my mind. He seems to have a very pragmatic viewpoint about my kids, and I believe him when he says he'll do what he can to help. But it's going to take a little time for me to start thinking of Tom as an ally instead of the enemy. By no stretch of the imagination did our conversation encompass enjoying myself."

"So stretch your legs instead and help me win. There's a prize for winning," he added craftily.

Kiley chuckled at his expression. "Well, why didn't you say so? I never could resist a prize."

"I'll remember that." His blue eyes twinkled with an answering laughter—and something else. Something too elusive to put a name to.

Kiley took her place at the crowded starting line.

She waved at Chris and Wayland farther down the line, pleased to see them taking part in the activities, and turned to Max.

"What do we do?"

Max gave her a pitying look. "Your memory must be failing. We'll simply use these to tie our legs together." He showed her the two lengths of twine he was holding. "Stand beside me. Closer," he ordered. "We have to be touching." He reached out and pulled her up against him.

Kiley felt the familiar surge of warmth flood her as his hard body pressed against her from calf to shoulder. What was racing was her heart, she thought ruefully as she felt her pulse speed up.

"Damn!" Max muttered. "This isn't going to work too well. You're too short."

"I am not." She looked down her nose at him. "My feet exactly reach the ground."

"Just what the world needs. Another Henny Youngman."

"You don't need twine. You need glasses."

"Quit stalling and hold still." Bending down, Max securely tied her left leg to his right one.

He eyed his handiwork dubiously then said, "Let's try a practice run." He moved forward, taking Kiley by surprise. She lost her balance and fell against him.

"Careful," he cautioned, steadying her.

Kiley's face was buried against his chest, and the sun-warmed smell of his clean skin overlaid by the tangy scent of his cologne teased her nostrils and drifted into her lungs, supercharging the air in them. She held her breath but succeeded only in pushing her sensitive breasts into him.

Eager to escape this subtle form of torture, Kiley jerked back, lost her balance and fell, bringing Max down on top of her.

She closed her eyes, trying to ignore the whole situation, but her lack of sight suddenly made her other senses intensely aware—aware of the pungent odor of the crushed grass beneath them, of the heat of the hot sun beating down on her face and of Max's heavy weight crushing her into the soft earth.

"Need any help there, Max?" A laughing voice penetrated Kiley's absorption and she winced.

"Go worry about your own strategy, Joe." Max slipped an arm under Kiley, and using his other arm as a brace, managed to get them both on their feet.

"Sorry," she muttered.

"Don't get discouraged yet," Max encouraged her.

Kiley chuckled. "When should I get discouraged? I'm afraid I'm just going to make you lose."

"I'd rather lose with you than win with someone else."

Kiley stared into Max's sparkling eyes, feeling slightly disoriented. His words had been delivered in a light teasing tone, but his eyes had reflected something else. The sun's getting to you, Kiley Sheridan, she told herself.

"Get ready!" a large man near the sidelines bellowed.

Max slipped an arm around Kiley's waist and held her against him. "We'll move our bound legs together on the count of one and our free ones on the count of two. Okay?"

"Sure." The word had a slightly breathless quality to it as the hand he was using to hold her up accidently brushed against her breast.

"Get set! Go!" the man yelled and the racers stumbled off the starting line.

"Careful, Kiley," Max warned as the pair to their left fell, tripping up the couples behind them and creating a huge pile of laughing bodies.

"That took care of a good chunk of the competition," Max said in satisfaction.

She laughed. "No, that took care of the bad chunk of the competition. And anyway, didn't your mother ever tell you it's not whether you win or lose, it's how you play the game that matters?"

"That's simply another way of saying that form is everything and substance nothing and I don't believe it. Go faster." Max pulled her closer to him, almost entirely supporting her weight as he urged her forward.

"I don't think so," Kiley objected.

"You can do it. Just concentrate on maintaining the rhythm."

"No, not that," Kiley said, panting as they began to pass the competition. "I was referring to your dismal view of good sportsmanship."

"Philosophy later, winning now." Max tightened his grip on her and increased their speed.

Kiley gasped as the hard bar of his forearm pushed up against her breasts, sending a wave of longing through her. She tried to concentrate on the end of the race as it came closer and closer.

"We won!" Max exuberantly hugged her as they crossed the finish line.

"Good job, Max," someone yelled.

"Hey, Max, I claim the lady for the wheelbarrow race," called a young man of about twenty-five who looked like he was training for the Mr. Universe contest.

"Go find your own partner, Ken," Max yelled back. "Kiley's mine."

Kiley felt a surge of pleasure at the possessiveness in Max's voice and it disturbed the last vestiges of her composure, because it was not how she normally reacted.

"Allow me to present the prize." The overweight man who'd started the race handed Kiley a large, beautifully wrapped box.

"Thank you." Kiley smiled warmly at him. "I'll . . ." She started to move to the seats and almost pitched forward. She had forgotten that she was still attached to Max.

He grabbed her, his fingers splaying across her abdomen, sending a sharp jab of electricity through her.

"Hey, Max, you can untie the poor thing," the bodybuilder said. "I promise not to steal her."

"Impudent kid," Max muttered as he leaned over and worked on the knots. "I'm beginning to think that I'm nurturing a pack of vipers."

"I think that particular one sounds more like he belongs to a pack of wolves." She watched in fascination as the brilliant sunlight gilded Max's dark hair with a fiery halo.

"There." Max tugged the final tie loose.

"Thanks. Let's go sit down and open up my prize."

"Our prize." Max followed her to a picnic table and sat beside her.

"Mine," she insisted. "You have a whole store to choose from. Someone did a fantastic job of wrapping this."

"Gift wrapping." Max crumpled the silver paper she was pulling off.

"Gift wrapping? Dawn . . ." Kiley paused, her face suddenly thoughtful. Wrapping gifts sounded like fun, and it wouldn't require much reading ability.

"Forget it." Max had no trouble interpreting her expression. "I'm not bumping one of our experienced people for a rank beginner."

"But—"

"Think a minute, Kiley. What kind of reaction is your student likely to get from her fellow workers if she's given a job that she not only hasn't earned, but that originally belonged to someone else? Someone who didn't voluntarily give it up? Her co-workers would resent her, which is hardly going to help her adjust."

"You're right, of course. It just seemed a shame not to take advantage of any job that didn't require much in the line of reading skills." She took the lid off the box. "Let's see what I've got. I'll bet . . ." Kiley blinked uncertainly as she pulled out a pastel pink plaster cherub about fifteen inches high. "What on earth . . ." She stared in disbelief at its abdomen. "It's got a clock in its belly!" she said incredulously.

"Yup, your cherub certainly does." Max gave her an innocent smile,.

"My cherub?" Kiley frowned at him. "A second ago you were claiming it."

"A second ago I hadn't seen it," Max said candidly.

"That's . . ." Kiley paused as she studied its smiling little face. "You know, Max, she looks kind of cheerful."

"So does a fifth of Scotch about a third of the way down, but that doesn't mean you should finish the bottle."

"Shh, you'll hurt her feelings."

"Her?" Max peered dubiously at the statue.

"All the best angels are girls," Kiley said blithely. "What shall I call her?"

"As seldom as possible," Max said dryly.

"What'd you win, Miss Sheridan?" Amad and David Mallings joined them.

"Priscilla." Kiley gestured toward the clock.

"Priscilla? It's kind of . . ." Amad eyed it dubiously.

"See, I told you," Max said in an audible aside to Kiley.

"Your lack of proper appreciation for Priscilla is undoubtedly caused by a deficiency in the masculine genetic code. No doubt the flaw is located on the same chromosome that makes men sit in front of a TV set and watch a bunch of grown men try to mangle each other on a football field," she said tartly.

"Well, if you like it, that's all that matters," Amad said, his tone clearly indicating he didn't understand how she could, but he was willing to accept it as a friend's foible.

"Miss Sheridan, this here is David Mallings. He's just started at the store, too." Amad introduced the young man beside him with a flourish.

Kiley tried to ignore the disquiet she felt at the frank hero worship reflected in Amad's face and turned to David.

"Good afternoon, David." She smiled politely at him.

"Miss Sheridan. Sir." David gave them a gleaming smile, displaying what Kiley was sure was the result of years of orthodontic work. "Actually you've got a real little treasure here, Miss Sheridan." He picked up the clock and examined it closely. "Victorian reproductions are all the rage. Miss Marsdon was showing this piece to some of us yesterday. It's a sample from a company in England."

"Clarissa Marsdon is one of our senior buyers," Max elaborated when Kiley looked at him questioningly.

"She says that it's going to be a real hot item for the Christmas trade," David added.

"Really?" Amad eyed the clock with new respect. "You mean people really want to buy something like that?"

Max chuckled. "I share your doubts, but if Clarissa says the public will buy it, they'll buy it. She's absolutely uncanny when it comes to knowing what people want."

"She sure is," David agreed. "Dad says he'd back Clarissa's instincts any day. Well, it was nice meeting you, Miss Sheridan." With another blinding smile, he left, followed by Amad.

"At least somebody appreciates Priscilla." She carefully put the cherub into the box.

"Come on." Max picked up the box with one hand and pulled Kiley to her feet with the other. "We'll put your gargoyle in the house and get something to eat. Maybe there will still be some of those tarts left."

"Maybe." She happily went along with him. It was turning out to be a truly wonderful day. Not only was she having a great time partnering Max, but her students also seemed to be enjoying themselves.

Wayland and Chris had been quickly absorbed into a large group of teenage boys who spent the afternoon alternating between the pool and the food tables.

Dawn had discovered a friend about her own age, and the pair of them spent their time happily taking part in the various activities while keeping an eye on the boys.

Jenny proved to be a focal point for a lot of women, and Tami was kept busy talking to all the people who came to admire the baby.

WITH REGRET, KILEY BEGAN to round up her students at six o'clock. She didn't want to leave. She wanted to stay where she was—with Max.

She felt a surge of pleasure as she watched him walk toward her across the driveway. His dark hair was windblown and his pale blue shirt and white shorts had grass stains on them. Probably from when she'd tripped him up before the race, she thought, then suddenly remembered her clock.

"My prize," she said.

"What did you have in mind?" Max whispered under cover of Dawn's and Tami's laughter as they buckled Jenny into her car seat.

"I was referring to Priscilla," she said repressively.

"Ah, yes, your gargoyle. We left it in the small sitting room, remember?"

Kiley turned to Wayland and said, "I'm going to get my clock. When Chris gets here with Amad, tell them wait. I'll be right back."

"I could go help Chris look for Amad," Wayland offered.

"No, thanks," Kiley said emphatically. "At least this way I know where three of you are."

Max put his arm around her shoulder and walked into the house with her. Kiley sighed as a feeling of almost euphoric contentment spread through her. She was pleasantly tired and well-fed, and Max's protective arm added the final touch—as if she was cherished. She savored the feeling all the more because she knew it wasn't true. Max might like her and she didn't doubt for a moment that he desired her, but cherishing was something else again. There wasn't a man in the world who cherished her, and the thought made her feel sad.

You're just tired and it's making you maudlin, she chided herself. You've got a good life. Concentrate on what you've got and not on what you don't.

"There she is." Max reached out and picked the silver-striped box off the table, then frowned.

# IT'S A WILD, WILD, WONDERFUL

# FREE OFFER!

## HERE'S WHAT YOU GET:

**1.** *Four New Harlequin Temptation® Novels—FREE!* Everything comes up hearts and diamonds with four exciting romances—yours FREE from Harlequin Reader Service®. Each of these brand-new novels brings you the passion and tenderness of too greatest love stories.

**2.** *A Lovely and Elegant Gold-Plated Chain—FREE!* You'll love y elegant 20k gold electroplated chain! The necklace is finely crafted with 160 double-soldered links and is electroplate finish in genuine 20k gold. And it's yours free as added thanks for giv our Reader Service a try!

**3.** *An Exciting Mystery Bonus—FREE!* You'll go wild over this surprise gift. It is attractive as well as practical.

**4.** *Free Home Delivery!* Join Harlequin Reader Service® and enjo the convenience of previewing 4 new books every month deliv to your home. Each book is yours for $2.39—26¢ less than the cover price. And there is no extra charge for postage and handling! If you're not fully satisfied, you can cancel at any tim just by sending us a note or shipping statement marked "cance or by returning any shipment to us at our cost. Great savings an total convenience are the name of the game at Harlequin!

**5.** *Free Newsletter!* It makes you feel like a partner to the world's most popular authors...tells about their upcoming books...eve gives you their recipes!

**6.** *More Mystery Gifts Throughout the Year!* No joke! Because ho subscribers are our most valued readers, we'll be sending you additional free gifts from time to time with your monthly shipments—as a token of our appreciation!

# GO WILD
## WITH HARLEQUIN TODAY—
## JUST COMPLETE, DETACH AND
## MAIL YOUR FREE-OFFER CARD!

# GET YOUR GIFTS FROM HARLEQUIN
## *ABSOLUTELY FREE!*

Mail this card today!

© 1990 HARLEQUIN ENTERPRISES LIMITED

PLACE
JOKER
STICKER
HERE

## PLAY THIS CARD RIGHT!

**YES!** Please send me my 4 Harlequin Temptation® novels FREE along with my free Gold-Plated Chain and free mystery gift. I wish to receive all the benefits of the Harlequin Reader Service® as explained on the opposite page.

142 CIH MDWB (U-H-T-06/90)

| | |
|---|---|
| NAME | (PLEASE PRINT) |
| ADDRESS | APT. |
| CITY | |
| STATE | ZIP CODE |

Offer limited to one per household and not valid to current Harlequin Temptation® subscribers. All orders subject to approval.

### HARLEQUIN READER SERVICE® "NO RISK" GUARANTEE

• There's no obligation to buy—and the free books remain yours to keep.
• You pay the low members-only price and receive books before they appear in stores.
• You may end your subscription anytime—just write and let us know or return any shipment to us at our cost.

# IT'S NO JOKE!

## MAIL THE POSTPAID CARD AND GET FREE GIFTS AND $10.60 WORTH OF HARLEQUIN NOVELS—*FREE!*

"What's wrong?" Kiley asked.

"The box feels..." He lifted the lid, looked inside and said, "Empty."

"Empty?" Kiley took the box from him and pulled out the crumpled tissue paper. There was no clock.

"Someone's kidnapped Priscilla!" she said disbelievingly.

"Someone *stole* Priscilla." Max's harsh voice cut through Kiley's anger. His face was set in hard lines, and his eyes were icy slits.

He glanced over the assortment of athletic bags people had brought to carry their swimming gear.

Kiley followed his glance, remembering that all three boys had brought battered gym bags embellished with the high school's distinctive logo.

One of them was still there.

"Wayland Riveras," Max read from the tag dangling from its handle, then picked it up as if testing its weight.

Kiley instinctively grabbed the bag, cradling it to her chest as if protecting both it and her students from Max's unvoiced yet clearly audible suspicions.

"Wayland is not a thief," she insisted.

"No, that bag is too light to have the clock in it. But where's Amad's?" He glanced through the stack of bags again.

"He probably left it out by the pool. Neatness is not a common teenage trait. And why are you just looking at my students' bags? What about all the rest of them?" she snapped.

"This is the first time anything has ever been stolen in all the years we've been holding this picnic," he said tightly.

"And so, of course, one of my students had to do it," Kiley spluttered, so angry she felt like smacking Max with the bag she was holding. How dare he leap to such an unfounded and totally unwarranted conclusion?

"Amad was the one eyeing the silver," Max defended himself.

"But not Priscilla," Kiley reminded him. "Priscilla didn't interest him at all. In fact, if I remember correctly, it was your fair-haired child from the suburbs who liked Priscilla."

"David?" Max eyed her incredulously. "Why would he steal a piece of Victoriana?"

"Why would Amad? Besides—" she took a deep breath and tried to restore some semblance of normality to a totally unreal situation "—we don't know for certain that Priscilla's even been stolen. Maybe somebody just took her out of the box to look at her and forgot to put her back."

"Sure," he scoffed. "And maybe peace is going to break out all over the world tomorrow."

"Well, I'd rather assume people are honest than convict them of something with no evidence whatsoever." She gave him an angry glare and stormed out of the house.

As she reached the car, she made an effort to appear unconcerned. She was determined not to ruin the day for her students by letting them know what had happened.

"Hey, that's my gym bag. Thanks, Miss Sheridan." Wayland took it from her and shoved it under the seat. "I meant to go back for it, then I forgot all about it."

"Where's Amad?" Kiley asked Chris, who was sitting in the car.

"Oh, he says he doesn't need a lift," Chris answered. "He said that David guy he was so chummy with this afternoon was taking a bunch of guys to his father's place and he invited Amad to go along."

"I see." Kiley pulled the sliding panel door closed and started toward the driver's side.

"Kiley." Max emerged from the house and called to her.

Kiley was unable to contain her anger. "Thanks for inviting us. We really enjoyed ourselves. You have no idea what an *enlightening* experience it was." She threw the words at him like darts.

She climbed into the driver's seat and drove away without another look at Max's frustrated face.

"Are you mad at Mr. Winthrop?" Dawn asked cautiously as they sped down the driveway.

Kiley lifted her foot off the gas pedal and asked, "Why would I be mad at him?"

"I don't know, but you were speeding and you never speed." Dawn turned and looked out the back window. "And he's still standing there watching us."

"I think he likes her," Tami said judiciously. "His eyes kinda smile when he looks at her."

"Of course he looks at her," Wayland said. "She's got a great bod—I mean . . ." He suddenly seemed to realize what he was saying. "If she weren't a teacher, she'd have a—"

Kiley laughed. "I'll accept the compliment in the spirit in which it was given, and we'll forget the exact wording. Now tell me what you thought of your fellow workers." The innocuous subject filled the conversation as they returned to town, but Kiley couldn't keep her thoughts from the devastating Max Winthrop or his accusations.

# 7

"GOOD MORNING." Kiley looked up from the notes she'd been studying as her students surged into the room and sat at the conference table. "I see you got home all right last night, Amad."

"Yeah, David has a brand new red Ferrari." Amad's voice was frankly envious. "And you should see his house. All the bedrooms have their own baths and the couches didn't have foam rubber cushions. They were full of feathers. Some day I'm going to have me a house full of nice stuff like that," he vowed.

"If you—" Kiley glanced at the door as a sudden silence descended on the room. Max was standing there, wearing one of the immaculately tailored gray suits of which he seemed to have an inexhaustible supply. His expression numbed Kiley's instinctive pleasure at seeing him. He had obviously heard what Amad had said and was no doubt drawing unpleasant conclusions about how Amad intended to achieve his goal.

Kiley raised her chin slightly and stared at him as if daring him to voice his suspicions. When he didn't say anything, she asked, "What may we do for you, Mr. Winthrop?"

"It's what I can do for you, Miss Sheridan." His voice was blessedly normal, even if his expression was still watchful. "Since I was coming this way anyway, Tom asked me to tell you that your students' orientation has been set back fifteen minutes."

"Thank you," Kiley murmured, wondering why Max had been coming this way. To see her? Or to check up on Amad? Or maybe his being at this end of the corridor had nothing to do with them at all. Maybe he hadn't given her or her students a thought since the picnic yesterday. Strangely enough, the idea didn't make her feel any better.

Kiley watched as Max took a seat at the end of the table. He smiled at the visibly wary students then turned to Amad. "That's a nice tie, Amad," he said.

Kiley shot Max a sharp glance, wondering what he was getting at. Surely the store wasn't missing a tie!

To her relief, Amad took the compliment at face value. He stroked his hand over the navy and deep-red striped tie. "It's real silk," he confided. "David's dad gave it to me last night."

"Oh?" Max's features looked no more than politely interested, but Kiley tensed, sensing a purpose behind the question.

"Uh-huh. Mr. Mallings told me that when he started, he only had one tie just like me, 'cept his was green and yellow. And he said Mr. Winthrop, the one before you, he gave him a new silk tie and told him that one day he'd be able to buy all the ties he wanted. That all he had to do was believe in himself and work like hell.

"Mr. Mallings said it was the best advice he ever got and it's as true for me today as it was for him then. And he gave me this tie and told me that someday I'd give a beginner a tie, too.

"And you know what else he said, Miss Sheridan?" Amad turned eagerly to her. "He said that he never went to college, either. That you can get on the management training program here by having worked in the store for at least three years and having two recommendations from your supervisors. That's what I'm going to do."

"Yeah." Wayland laughed. "Pretty soon we'll all be calling you Mr. Varia."

"Good for you, Amad." Kiley gave Max a satisfied nod. But instead of looking apologetic, Max merely looked thoughtful.

A muted buzz signaled the fact that the main doors had been opened. Kiley surreptitiously glanced at the door, wondering where Bubba was. He'd missed the picnic and now he was late for his first day of work. That wasn't like him, but there wasn't anything she could do about it. She had the other five eager employees to worry about. To say nothing of Max, who seemed quite content to stay where he was.

Deciding to make good use of the unexpected time, she said, "Since we've got an extra fifteen minutes, we'll work on possible problems you might run across in the store."

She shot a quick glance at Max. At least he was watching her instead of poor Amad.

"We're going to try a role-playing technique in which we act out our various situations."

"Act out?" Wayland asked dubiously.

"It's a widespread technique," Kiley assured him. "In fact I once read an article about a famous author who said that whenever she had an interview coming up, she'd list the ten questions she absolutely didn't want to be asked and then practice an answer for them."

"But what good does that do?" Dawn demanded.

"If you have a chance to practice your response to trying situations, you're less likely to say something you shouldn't or lose your temper," Kiley explained. "It's kind of like when you haven't done your homework and you try out all kinds of creative reasons for not having it."

"Oh." Dawn ducked her head guiltily.

"Now then, Tami, you be the customer, and Chris, you be the clerk. The rest of us are going to observe. We'll pretend that the store had advertised a special on, say, winter blankets and Tami has come downtown to buy one. When she tries to purchase it, Chris will tell her there aren't any left. Chris, you start things off." Kiley nodded encouragingly at him.

"Good morning, madam. May I help you?" Chris said politely.

"Yes, I want to buy one of those blankets you got on sale. In pink."

"We don't have any left."

"Then I'll take blue."

"No, we haven't got any left in any color."

"What do you mean, you don't got any left?" Tami threw herself into the role with all the enthusiasm of a young Sarah Bernhardt. "It's ten o'clock in the morning. The store just opened. How can you be sold out already?"

"Well . . ."

"Listen, mister, I got up early, came across town on the bus—it took two transfers—just to buy this blanket and you tell me that you're out of them! What kind of rip-off is this?"

"This isn't a rip-off—" Chris began.

"Then where's my blanket?"

"How about another brand?" Chris asked in inspiration.

"Is it on sale?"

"Well, no, but—"

"Aha! Bait and switch!" Tami exclaimed triumphantly, while Max buried his head in his hands and moaned.

"What's bait and switch?" Dawn asked.

"We learned about it in a class on modern living I took last semester," Tami explained. "It's when a store advertises somethin' at a real low price and when you try to buy it, they tell you they're out of it, but they have something even better, only it's always more expensive."

"Okay." Kiley took control of the conversation. "Let's analyze what happened."

"I got an unreasonable customer," Chris complained.

"They come with the territory," Max said ruefully.

"But what went wrong with this customer?" Kiley persisted. "Or, more specifically, with the situation?"

"It was all downhill after 'may I help you?'" Amad offered.

"Precisely." Kiley gave him an approving look. "Now the question is why."

"Because the store didn't have what she wanted," Wayland said.

"Exactly. And then what happened?"

Chris grimaced. "She got mad."

"And you tried to respond to her anger instead of to the situation," Kiley pointed out. "In essence, you let her dictate the course of the conversation. What you should have done was to have kept the focus on the blanket she wanted to buy. Let's try it again using what we've learned. Tami has just come in and asked for the blanket. Chris doesn't have any left. What can he say?" She glanced around the conference table.

"He could tell her why they don't have any left," Wayland suggested. "My mom doesn't get half as mad about things if you tell her why you did it."

"Good. Try it, Chris."

"I'm sorry, madam, but the shipment hasn't come in yet," Chris said.

"Now, what else can he do to placate this customer?" Kiley asked.

"Once when I tried to buy a record Winthrops had on sale, they were sold out and the clerk gave me a rain check to buy it at the sale price when the new shipment came in," Dawn offered. "Chris could do that."

"Very good." Max's unexpected praise sent a warm flush over Dawn's pale face. "It's store policy to always honor sale prices. You have the customer fill out one of the postcards we keep by all the cash registers, and tell them you'll mail it to them when the item comes in. You'll be taught all this in your sales training, but you have excellent ideas."

"But what about my bus transfers?" Tami persisted.

"If the customer had trouble getting to the store, we'll waive the normal delivery fee and deliver the item to her home," Max said.

"Okay." Kiley glanced at the clock. "We have a minute to recap. What is of paramount importance when dealing with a customer's problem?"

"We should try to fix the problem and not get angry at the customer," Amad said.

"Very well put." Kiley nodded in satisfaction. "We'll start our regular sessions tomorrow at nine-fifty. Good luck with your orientation today. If you should need me for any reason, I'll be in my office."

"Bye, Miss Sheridan." They trooped out, leaving Kiley and Max in the small conference room. A room that suddenly seemed to become much smaller as the force of Max's personality filled the void.

"That's a very interesting technique you just used, and probably a lot more effective than the lectures Tom favors," Max said thoughtfully.

"Thank you." Kiley felt a warm glow at his unqualified praise. If only he'd extend some of it to Amad.

"In fact, I'd like to see some more of it."

"Day after tomorrow at our regular session," she said promptly, pleased to have him attend. The better he got to know her students, the better he'd like them. And the quicker he'd come to realize just how ridiculous his suspicions about Amad were.

"I'll be there, but what I really came by for was to tell you that your clock didn't surface last night when the caterers cleaned up."

"I see." Kiley studied his face, wondering if he was going to say anything more. Somehow, hearing his suspicions would make them seem more threatening. To her relief, he didn't.

"I've told Clarissa to hold one for you when the Christmas shipment arrives, but that won't be for several months yet."

"It's not necessary—"

"You were a guest in my house when it was stolen," Max bit out. "And I want you to have it."

"All right, thank you. I appreciate it," Kiley said, wanting to end the conversation about the theft.

Max stood and started toward the door. "Oh, by the way, when Bubba arrives, would you try to explain to him that most employers prefer their employees to be on time."

"Certainly," Kiley said calmly, even though what she really wanted to do was to shriek in frustration. The theft of her clock had created tension, and Bubba had added to it by deciding to operate on his own time schedule.

He might be ill. She frowned as the thought suddenly occurred to her. But from what Amad had said yesterday, it didn't sound like it. She'd give him another hour, then she'd try calling his home, she decided as she gathered her papers.

The phone call wasn't necessary. Thirty minutes later Bubba stuck his head into her office, and said, "Can I talk to you a minute, Miss Sheridan?"

"Bubba! Where have you been? Is anything wrong? Hello, Brenda," she added when she caught sight of the young woman behind him.

"Hi, Miss Sheridan." Brenda gave her a sunny smile.

"I got great news, Miss Sheridan." Bubba leaned on her desk while Brenda sat in the chair beside it. "Mookie Wallingford got a scholarship to Notre Dame."

"That is good news," Kiley agreed, mentally scrambling to identify Mookie Wallingford. She drew a blank, which wasn't really surprising. She knew very few students who could qualify academically for Notre Dame.

"I can't seem to place the name," she admitted when Bubba waited, obviously expecting more of a reaction.

"That's probably because you never met him," Bubba said patiently.

Kiley hid a grin. "That's probably it. Why don't you explain the whole thing to me again?"

"Sure. You remember I didn't get that track scholarship to Western because I was their fifth choice and they only had four grants to award this year?"

"Uh-huh." Kiley nodded encouragingly.

"Mookie Wallingford was one of the four who got a scholarship, but he really wanted to go to Notre Dame. When they didn't offer him a scholarship, he accepted Western. Well, on Friday one of Notre Dame's men signed a pro baseball contract, which left their track team a man short. So they offered the place to Mookie. He grabbed at the chance."

"Which left Western short a man," Kiley realized.

"Yup, and I got the spot." Bubba beamed at her. "I get to run track for four more years."

"Bubba, that's fantastic!" Kiley grinned happily at him.

"Yeah, it is, isn't it? My mom spent the weekend calling all my relatives, even my Aunt Sue who she hasn't spoken to in five years. I'm the first person in my family to ever go to college."

"And you'll do them all proud," Kiley said, sending up a silent prayer to make it true.

"So, you see, if I'm going to college, I won't be needing a job here."

"True," Kiley agreed, reviewing her list of graduating seniors to see who could take his place. The process came to an abrupt halt when Bubba gestured toward Brenda and said, "Since Brenda here doesn't have a job lined up, she said she'd like to talk to you about it." He straightened. "Well, thanks for everything, Miss Sheridan. I'll be seeing you. I still got to tell coach."

"Good luck, Bubba. If you get a chance, stop in from time to time and let me know how you're getting along, okay?"

"I will. Bye."

Kiley turned to Brenda and said, "I thought you were going to be spending the summer with your dad in California."

"I was, but he got married again. Kind of unexpectedly." Brenda grimaced. "She's twenty-two and she called and suggested that I might want to put off visiting Dad until they've had a chance to settle down to married life, was how she put it."

"Hmm. It can be a little rough at first when you're trying to blend families," Kiley said comfortingly.

"From how my dad's new wife talked, I don't think she's going to try," Brenda said ruefully. "I think I'm going to find that I'll only see my father when he comes to the east coast."

"That's too bad, but don't let your new stepmother push you out. Remember, he's your father."

"That's what Mom says, but, you know, my folks have been divorced for so long that he doesn't really seem like my father. I mean, I like him and all, but it's not as if it was my mom telling me to get lost. Anyway." Brenda took a deep breath. "This whole thing has kind of messed up my plans. You see, Mom already accepted an assignment from the hotel chain to set up a resort in Greece, thinking I'd be spending the summer with Dad. She said I could come along to Greece with her, but I know she'll be so busy that I'd never see her, and besides, I think it's time I started to think about the future."

"Sounds reasonable to me." Kiley nodded encouragingly.

"Mom wants me to go to college, but I hate the idea. It would be a constant struggle to get everything done on time, and it's not like there's anything I want to train for."

"Have you explained how you feel to your mother?"

"Uh-huh. Last night when I ran into Bubba at the movies, he told me how he wasn't going to need his job here at Winthrops. It sounds like something I would enjoy doing and could do well," Brenda said enthusiastically. "I like working with people, and I'm really good at predicting fashion trends."

Kiley grinned. "I'll say. You were the first person in my sixth-hour class to wear neon socks."

"In the whole school," Brenda said complacently. "Anyway, Mom said that if I got hired, I could stay with Grandma and try it for the summer and we'd reassess the situation in the fall. So, can I have the job?" Brenda eyed her eagerly.

"The final decision isn't mine to make, Brenda. It's Mr. Winthrop's." And after the disappearance of the Victorian clock, he might jump at the chance of reducing the number of her students in his store, Kiley thought glumly.

"When can you ask him?" Brenda asked. "Mom's due to leave for Greece on Friday and I'd like to get everything settled beforehand so she won't worry."

"I'll talk to Mr. Winthrop today and call you tonight, one way or the other," Kiley promised.

"Thanks, Miss Sheridan. I really appreciate this. Bye."

"Bye." Kiley absently closed the door behind her as she considered the best time to approach Max. She decided the end of the day would be best. The theft of her clock wouldn't be quite so fresh in his mind.

She was determined to get Brenda this job. Not so much for Brenda's sake. Brenda was a bright, personable teenager with a large, relatively wealthy family who would make sure she never lacked for anything. No, Kiley needed Brenda for the sake of the program.

To drive home to Max that learning disabilities affected all social and economic levels.

Kiley spent the day carefully plotting her strategy, then took the precaution of stopping by personnel on her way to Max's office to make sure nothing had happened involving her students.

Tom wasn't in his office, but his secretary was able to tell her that it had been a totally uneventful day as far as her students were concerned. Feeling a little more confident, Kiley headed for Max's office.

She found Aggie engrossed at her computer screen.

"Good afternoon." Kiley smiled at her. "Is Max in?"

"He just returned a few minutes ago from measuring those amaryllis plants."

"And is no doubt planning new strategy." Kiley's lips twitched. "I'll have to buy him his own grow light, since he seems so keen to get his hands on Jane's."

"Might as well—" Aggie grinned "—because he's never going to find hers."

"Oh?" Kiley eyed her curiously. "Why's that?"

"Because a man never has been and never will be the equal of a determined woman."

"That just goes to show what you two know," Max said from the open door of his office. "Hi, Kiley, I thought I heard you out here trading treasonous thoughts with Aggie." He gave Kiley a slow smile. "I was just about to call you."

Her excitement intensified as she walked into his office. Max had been about to call her. Why, she wondered. Something work related? Or something personal? As she watched, he pressed his thumb and forefinger against the bridge of his nose as if trying to shut out pain.

"Bad day?" A surge of tenderness softened her voice.

"A perfect bitch of a day." Max sank down in the chair behind his desk, leaned his head back and closed his eyes. "And to cap it all off I just got off the phone with one of our British suppliers who tells me that there's a bitter labor strike at the mill in Scotland, which is threatening the availability of a popular line of winter woolens we sell."

"Good." She perched on the edge of his desk in front of him.

"Good!" Max opened one bright blue eye and peered at her. "What's the matter with you? Have you no compassion in your soul?"

"I'd rather have clothes in the right season."

"And now you're talking gibberish." Max nodded sagely. "It's been that kind of day."

"I'm not talking gibberish. I'm complaining."

"I got a lot of that today, too," Max said glumly.

"About the way stores sell things." She ignored his comment. "I mean, here it is early June, and you're already worried about a shipment of winter woolens. When was the last time you tried to buy a swimsuit in August?"

"Swimsuits should be bought at the start of the season," Max said repressively.

"You mean when they first appear in the stores in January," she said scathingly. "Who's thinking about swimsuits when it's freezing outside?"

"Oh, you'd be amazed." Max slowly studied her soft curves, and Kiley could almost feel his gaze touching her with feather-light strokes—heating her breasts and making the nipples convulse into tight, aching buds. She closed her eyes in negation of the unexpected feeling, but that only seemed to make her more aware of the lassitude spreading through her.

"And what about children?" she forced out, trying to keep to the neutral subject of retailing.

"Oh, I'm all in favor of children." His voice deepened perceptibly, and Kiley swallowed uneasily. "In fact," he continued, "I like children from start to finish. Especially from the start." His eyes slipped over her abdomen, and her body jerked as if she'd just touched a live wire.

Kiley blinked, uncertain of what was happening to her. They'd started out discussing the vagaries of retailing and somehow wound up with her emotions in turmoil. Did Max realize the effect he was having on her? The gleam in his eye made her suspect that he did, and that fact stiffened her pride as nothing else could.

"I was referring to the nasty habit children have of growing in the middle of the season, but anyway, this is all irrelevant," she said.

"Children?" He gave her a look of mock horror. "Children are never irrelevant."

"Speaking of children, did you find Jane's grow light?" she gibed.

"No, she probably carries it around with her," he grumbled. "But you're right. She's certainly behaving childishly."

Kiley swallowed a giggle at his aggrieved expression. "She isn't the only one."

"Et tu, Brutus? It's bad enough Aggie probably warns Jane before I leave the office, but that you should turn on me, too . . ."

"Women tend to stick together," she said unrepentently. "And speaking of being together . . ." She paused, mentally groping for the best way to present Brenda's case to him.

"Why do I have the feeling that you're about to make my headache worse?" Max asked dryly.

"Do you really have a headache?"

"A beaut. I told you, it's been an awful day. The shoplifters I'm used to, but the lady who stopped by the infants' department on her way to the hospital . . ." He shook his head disbelievingly.

Kiley frowned. "Why the hospital?"

"To have the baby she was nine months pregnant with."

"Wait a minute. Why would any sane person make a side trip to a department store on her way to the delivery room?"

"I never said she was sane." Max fingered the small purplish bruise under his left eye. "According to her husband, it was all our fault because we advertised the sale."

"The sale?" Kiley parroted.

"On christening gowns. Forty percent off, starting today."

"Keep going," Kiley ordered.

"It seems that she had her heart set on this hand-made, French lawn gown that was beyond her budget, but it became affordable at forty percent off. She was planning on being here when the store opened at ten. So when she went into labor early this morning, she decided to stop by here and pick it up on her way to the hospital. She said she figured she had lots of time because first babies take a while to arrive."

"But that's on average."

"Apparently she never heard of the laws governing averages. And to make matters worse, there was a huge crowd in the infant's department and she had to wait in line to pay. Fortunately, one of the store's security people saw her behaving in what he thought was a strange manner, and he called me."

"What'd you do?" Kiley asked in fascination.

"I called an ambulance and told her we'd be more than happy to hold the gown for her."

"And?"

"And that's when she suddenly smacked me with her purse. She told me she wasn't going anywhere without that gown. At that point I told her to take the damn thing with my compliments, just go to the hospital."

"Did she?"

"She was still arguing the matter when the paramedics showed up. They were a lot more persuasive than I was, which was a good thing. When I called the hospital later to check on her, they said she'd had the baby in the ambulance."

"That was probably why she was so irritable, because she was in transition," Kiley said thoughtfully.

"If that's a euphemism for nuts, I agree with you."

"You poor soul, you have had a miserable day, haven't you? But look on the bright side. You could have had a fire or an armed robber or . . ."

"Or the news you came down here to tell me?" Max eyed her speculatively.

"My news?" she said innocently.

"You remember. What you came to tell me that you can't seem to spit out."

"Nonsense," she said briskly. "It's quite simple." Kiley leaned toward him in her eagerness to convince him. "Bubba unexpectedly got a track scholarship so he doesn't need the job, and I wanted to tell you about the woman I've picked to take his place."

Max's expression wasn't enthusiastic, but neither did he flatly refuse to hire another of her students, as she'd feared. Encouraged, she continued.

"When I drew up my list of people to hire, I thought Brenda was going to be spending the summer with her father in California, but her plans changed at the last minute, so she's available."

"Tell me," Max said slowly, "would you have recommended her for a job originally if you'd known she was going to be here?"

"No, but not for the reason you're thinking. I made a tactical error with that list," Kiley admitted. "I didn't consider kids like Brenda because they have families willing and able to help them. Brenda's father is a dentist in California, and her mother is an executive who specializes in setting up new hotels. When I was choosing candidates, I stuck to kids who either had a severe physical problem, like Chris, or whose problems were more socioeconomic, because I saw their needs as greater. The result is that you've got the idea that learning disabled kids are strictly inner city, and they aren't."

"I know that," Max insisted. "Tell me about Brenda. What is her specific problem?"

"She actually has two: attention deficit and sequential problems. It's as if, when the teacher is talking to the class, Brenda's mind gives equal weight to everything she hears—the car driving down the street outside the classroom window, someone walking down the corridor, the kid in the seat next to her who's shuffling papers. Her mind doesn't have the faculty to automatically filter out inconsequential noises like an average person's does. Over the years she's learned coping techniques, so dealing one on one with a customer won't be a problem."

"And the sequential problems?"

"She can't follow a set of directions in her head," Kiley explained.

"Give me an example."

"If I were to say to you, get out of your chair, go to the window, check to see if there's a car outside, then write the color of it down on the pad beside the phone, you could do that. Brenda would make it to the window, then she'd be lost. However, her reading and writing skills in both English and French were at college graduate level when she entered the ninth grade. Which has allowed us to use the simple technique of writing things down and referring to the list as she goes."

"Sounds logical." Max nodded. "And I can't see any reason it won't work."

"Then you'll hire her?" Kiley held her breath.

"Yes," Max said, watching pleasure light her expressive features. What was it about her that made him agree to hire yet another one of her students when he was relatively certain that one of them was already indulging in petty theft? But when he looked at her, all he could think about was making her happy. He found it an extremely unsettling situation. Never before had he had any trouble separating business from pleasure. But Kiley was infiltrating all areas of his life, and he wasn't sure where it was going to end. All he knew for certain was that making her happy was more important to him than the fact that one of her protégés had probably used his hospitality to rip him off.

Giving in to the almost compulsive urge to touch her, he reached out and gently pulled her into his lap.

Startled, Kiley tensed as she landed against him. He was so close to her that the tips of her breasts were almost touching the smooth polished wool of his light gray suit jacket, and the heat from his body was sending out elusive tendrils of heat to ensnare her senses.

She tipped her head against his shoulder and stared into his gleaming eyes. "Why did you do that?" she asked.

"An irresistible impulse?" Max adjusted her slight weight more comfortably on his lap. His action made her graphically aware of the effect she was having on his body, and the knowledge pleased her.

"You don't strike me as the impulsive type."

"You bring out all sorts of latent characteristics," he said slowly. "For example, right now I feel like a sex maniac."

"Oh?" Kiley wiggled slightly, grinding her soft buttocks into his manhood. "I thought you had a headache."

"You don't." He gave her a hopeful look that sent a surge of tenderness through her.

"No, I don't, do I?"

With slow deliberation, she clasped the nape of his neck and tugged his head forward, sighing in anticipation as his lips came closer.

A sound of intense satisfaction escaped her as his lips met hers. Liquid fire seemed to flow through her veins as he shaped his mouth to hers and pressed slightly, demanding admission. Her mouth opened and his tongue surged inside, teasing hers.

She groaned and slipped a finger between two of the buttons on his white shirt to touch his skin beneath. She rubbed back and forth, savoring the warmth of his hair-roughened chest. Her fingers deftly worked two buttons free, and she slipped her whole hand inside, pressing her palm flat against his chest. His thick pelt of hair rubbed across her palm, and the heavy throb of his heartbeat was absorbed into her flesh. Her own heart lurched into an erratic beat as if trying to adjust itself to the rhythm of his. He felt so good, so absolutely right beneath her exploring fingertips.

"My poor wounded lamb," she murmured, gently touching the small purplish bruise with the tip of her tongue. Max jerked in reaction, and Kiley smiled with intense satisfaction. Somehow, the fact that he could send her emotions into turmoil didn't seem quite so threatening when she could do the same thing to him.

His hands, which had been holding her tight against him, slid up her back to her shoulders, and he gently eased them apart. "You're turning me into one gigantic ache," he said ruefully. "The only good thing about it is that it sure took my mind off my headache."

Kiley grinned at him. "Would you care to try for a cure?"

Max heaved a sigh that seemed to come from the very depths of his soul. "I make it a habit never to practice folk medicine in a room without a lock on the door."

Kiley laughed and got to her feet. "I'll file that away under things to be considered later." And continued, she decided.

# 8

"SCALO . . . SCALO . . . SCALOPPINI?" Dawn forced the word out.

"Perfect," Kiley enthused, "absolutely perfect. Another week and you'll be reading the whole menu."

"Yeah, I'm doing pretty good, ain't I?" Dawn said with a nonchalance that couldn't quite hide her glow of triumph. "And once I can read the whole menu—"

"You can serve the food instead of cooking it." Wayland finished what was obviously an oft-repeated phrase.

"Oh, you're just jealous because you don't like measuring people's feet," Dawn shot back.

Wayland glumly eyed the bandage on his thumb. "It's not the feet I mind. It's the other end. Who'da ever thought a kid's teeth could be so dangerous?"

"Ain't nothin' wrong with kids, provided you're smart enough to handle them. They—" Tami broke off as the door to the conference room opened.

Kiley looked up and a shimmer of pleasure skittered through her at the sight of Max standing in the doorway. He was wearing what she privately thought of as his business face, calm and remote. Had he come about something specific or was he merely here to observe her class again, she wondered. He'd attended almost a third of them in the past two weeks, and she still wasn't sure why he came. She hoped it was as much to see her as it was to see what she was accomplishing with her students. Her hope was bolstered by the fact that he invariably sat and had a cup of coffee with her once the class was over and her students had left for their regular jobs. They'd usually start out discussing what her students were doing then move on to subjects that had nothing to do with either her students or the store.

Max Winthrop was a very intelligent man with a wide range of interests, which she enjoyed exploring. But did he enjoy their conversations as much as she did? It was a question she had no answer to, but she comforted herself with the fact that he didn't have to stay after her students left. Come to that, he didn't have to come to her classes in the first place.

"Good morning, Mr. Winthrop," Kiley said, then winced as she caught the wry look Wayland shot Amad at her formality. Did everyone know about her growing fascination with Max? Honestly, she thought with a touch of asperity, one had about as much privacy as a fish in a fishbowl around this place.

"Good morning." Max's smile enveloped them all. He perched on the edge of the conference table beside her, and Kiley's eyes were drawn to the way the polished gray fabric stretched across his heavy-muscled thighs. Longing twisted through her and she tore her gaze away, telling herself that her reaction was inappropriate to the workplace. Unfortunately, she seemed totally unable to assign Max to a neat slot and have him stay there. He was much too vibrant a personality to remain locked in place.

Kiley glanced at her watch. "We've got ten minutes left. Does anyone have anything to discuss?"

"We could discuss how Wayland didn't handle that poor child," Tami snipped.

"Poor child!" Wayland glared at her. "I'm the one who had to get a tetanus shot and I'll probably have a scar."

"Maybe we should talk about how to handle kids," Kiley said thoughtfully. "How about if I act out the part of the mother, Brenda, you be the sales clerk, and—"

"And I'll be the kid," Max unexpectedly said.

"You?" Kiley eyed him uncertainly. Anyone less childlike she'd yet to meet.

"Certainly. You can't cope with a kid if he isn't represented, and since I've been trying to cope with them since I first came to work here when I was fourteen—"

"You started working here when you were fourteen?" Amad asked incredulously.

"Uh-huh, after school and on weekends. Not that I got paid," Max said ruefully. "My dad told me that it was illegal to pay someone under sixteen, and I believed him."

"Yeah, my dad claims it's immoral for him to pay me to mow the lawn," Chris commiserated.

"Now then," Kiley inserted before they started trading stories and wasted the ten minutes. "I am shopping for—"

"Anything but shoes," Wayland muttered.

"Picture frames. Pretend this is one." Max picked up her notepad and handed it to her. Then he moved one of the heavy conference chairs away from the table. "This chair is the cash register. Brenda, you stand behind it. Miss Sheridan is about to pay for the frame she wants with a credit card."

Once Brenda was in place, Kiley started toward the make-believe cash register, only to stop when Max started in another direction. "How old are you supposed to be?" Kiley suddenly asked.

"Three." Max gave her an angelic smile. "And I hate shopping."

"I see." Kiley reached out, took his hand and pulled him toward her. He came, reluctantly.

"I want to go home!" Max howled, throwing himself into his role with a great deal of enthusiasm.

"We will, just as soon as Mommy pays for the frame." Kiley tugged him toward the waiting Brenda.

"I want to go home *now*." Max's voice rose belligerently.

"In a minute." Kiley handed Brenda the notepad and let go of Max's hand to take a credit card out of her purse.

"Go home now, now, now." Max punctuated the litany with a series of kicks to the base of the chair.

Kiley frowned quellingly at Max and handed her credit card to Brenda.

Max ignored her, continuing to kick the chair. It jumped forward.

"Um, ma'am, do you know your kid's kicking my cash register?" Brenda offered tentatively.

"He just needs a nap." Kiley borrowed the excuse a friend of hers had been using to explain her child's bad behavior for the past seven years.

"Mine." Max reached out and snatched the credit card Brenda was using.

"Hey!" Brenda grabbed for it.

"Don't do that," Wayland warned.

At the same instant Max captured Brenda's hand and said, "You are being bitten. Now what?"

"Madam!" Brenda turned to Kiley.

After one look at the gleeful expression on Max's face, Kiley muttered, "Oh, dear."

"You let go." Brenda tried to escape, but Max held on. "You let go or I'm going to smack you," Brenda finally said in frustration.

"I think we have reached an impasse." Kiley brought the proceedings to a halt. "Let's analyze what went wrong."

"Everything went wrong," Brenda muttered as she retreated to her seat.

"Then let's start at the beginning," Kiley said.

"You mean when Brenda told you that Mr. Winthrop was kicking the counter?" Tami asked. "What was wrong with that? He was."

"True," Max said, "but the mother had to have known it. She was standing right there. She was simply unwilling or unable to deal with her kid's behavior."

"So what was I supposed to do about it?" Brenda asked.

"Nothing," Max said. "You should have processed the charge and ignored the behavior. You should only interfere if what the child is doing is liable to hurt him. For example, if he had been kicking one of the plate glass mirrors, he could have slit an artery."

"We should be so lucky." Wayland rubbed his bandaged finger.

Max gave him a quelling look and turned to Brenda. "In that case, you should ask the mother to stop him."

"Yeah, but what if she doesn't?" Amad asked. "It seems to me that if she had any control over the kid, he wouldn'ta been doing it in the first place. I mean, my mom woulda smacked me good if I'da ever acted like that in a store."

"If the mother either can't or won't restrain the child, then you call your supervisor," Max said. "We don't want anyone hurt in one of our stores."

"Do you have all that much trouble with kids?" Kiley asked curiously.

"Not really. We see a lot of tired, cranky ones who should be home playing instead of being dragged around a store," Max said. "Your best bet is to try to remain aloof from their behavior and to keep telling yourself they'll outgrow it.

"Oh, by the way, Tami." Max turned to her. "You did a good job spotting the stolen credit card yesterday. You should have a check from the credit card company by the end of the month, and the store gift certificate will be in your paycheck on Friday."

"Thanks." Tami's face glowed with pride.

"What happened, Tami?" Kiley asked curiously.

"Some lady bought a whole bunch of stuff and she gave me a credit card to pay for it, and when I ran it through the little machine that checks numbers, it came back with the code for a stolen card."

"So what'd you do?" Kiley asked.

"Just what Mr. Preston said. I told the lady that the machine wasn't working and that I had to use one in the back of the department. Then I went to a phone and called security."

"They told us about it when we was orientated," Wayland elaborated. "The national credit card companies will pay you fifty bucks if you get back one of their stolen cards and the store'll give you a matching gift certificate."

"And they arrested the lady?" Kiley asked.

"No, she must'a realized I was on to her because the minute I was out of sight, she took off. And you know, she didn't look at all like a thief," Tami said slowly. "She looked like somebody's mother."

"The first requirement for a thief is that he not look like one," Max said, and his gaze swung to Amad for a fraction of a second before returning to Tami.

Kiley felt her heart sink. Max hadn't mentioned the missing clock for over a week, and she'd hoped that he'd finally realized how ridiculous his suspicions of Amad had been, but apparently he hadn't.

Eager to remove Amad from Max's presence, she said, "That's all for today. I'll see you all tomorrow, and when Mr. Preston gets back from vacation we can ask him to give us some more tips on how to handle kids."

"With a whip and a chain," Wayland muttered as he left.

Max chuckled. "That sounds like a crusty old bachelor in the making."

"Speaking of making things, I don't like the way you're trying to make Amad into a thief," Kiley said once they were alone.

"Did you know that an expensive electronic timing device for runners disappeared out of his department late yesterday afternoon?"

"What!"

"From a locked case. A case for which Amad had a key."

"Well, what about his supervisor? Surely he had a key, too?"

"The supervisor was at a department head meeting, and the other clerk was on break, which left Amad alone in the department for almost half an hour."

"Why are you so sure it was stolen then?" Kiley demanded.

"Because the supervisor replaced some things in the case before he left for the meeting, and right before five a customer asked to see the timer and it was gone."

"Maybe Amad sold it." Kiley groped for a logical explanation.

"I checked. There were no entries on the cash register tape that matched the price of the timer."

"I don't care what your cash register tape says, Amad didn't steal anything," Kiley insisted. "What was his explanation for all this?"

"He said that he showed several people things out of the case, but he didn't leave a customer there alone. Nor does he remember seeing the timer when he was getting things out of the case."

"Then maybe your supervisor made a mistake," Kiley bit out. "Why should it automatically be Amad who's at fault?"

"Amad is new, and that supervisor's been with us for twenty-seven years. Twenty-seven years with a spotless record."

"Amad is not a thief." Kiley spaced the words emphatically. "He's a young man who's had damned few breaks up until now, and I'm not going to let anyone spoil things for him because of some flimsy circumstantial evidence that probably has a simple explanation."

"Such as?" Max asked skeptically.

"I don't know . . . yet."

"Kiley." Max reached out and took her hand in his. His warm fingers closed around her chilled ones, sending a surge of tingling warmth through her. And that made her even angrier. How could her body react to him with such fervor when she was so mad at him? It made no sense. Not that anything seemed to be making much sense at the moment, she thought grimly.

"Kiley," Max repeated, "one of the first things you learn about working with people is that you can't win them all. Some of them are going to disappoint you."

"What do you plan to do?" Kiley asked apprehensively.

"For the moment, nothing. But when I can prove my suspicions . . ." His threat was all the more ominous for being unstated.

"I see." Kiley let out her breath on a long, shuddering sigh. She had some time to prove Amad innocent. But what could she do? If there was a thief, she decided, maybe she could figure out who it was. Max obviously wouldn't be looking for another thief—he believed he'd found the culprit.

"Max?" Kiley peered into his worried blue eyes, taking heart from the fact that he didn't like the situation any better than she did. "Will you promise me one thing? Will you promise to tell me before you take any action against Amad?"

"All right." Max nodded. "I promise. Now that that's settled, will you have lunch with me?"

"I'd love to," she said promptly, glad to shelve her concern over Amad for at least a few minutes.

"Well, since that was so easy, how about this Friday night?" he said promptly.

"What about this Friday night?"

"A friend called this morning to invite me to a birthday party she's giving for her husband. I'd like you to come with me."

"I see," Kiley said slowly, busily reviewing her wardrobe. She dismissed her few evening dresses as unequal to a party one of Max's friends might give. But there was that gorgeous jade silk gown she'd seen up in the limited editions room yesterday. It was equal to something worn at Buckingham Palace, and the color would do wonders for her skin.

"And if I know Marcia the party will be packed with Washington area business people," Max added, when Kiley, still lost in her plans, remained silent. "Think of all the opportunities for badgering some poor, unsuspecting soul about jobs for your students."

"I'd love to come," Kiley said, realizing he was right. A high-society party would be an excellent opportunity to make useful contacts for her students. She stole a quick glance at him as a depressing thought hit her. Had Max invited her not because he wanted her company, but because he wanted to redirect her crusade for jobs at some other business people?

No, she decided. Max might be incensed about the thefts, but it didn't appear to have affected his feelings toward her. He still liked her. Liked her a lot. There was no way she could mistake both the fervor and the tenderness behind the kisses they'd shared. Nor had he ever made any attempt to disguise the fact that he enjoyed their conversations, even when they disagreed. There were so many areas where they operated on the same wavelength that it made his stubborn refusal to see the truth about Amad all the more frustrating. But he would, she vowed. She'd make him realize how wrong he was if she had to catch the thief herself.

It wasn't until after class two days later that Kiley was able to talk to Amad without being obvious about it. She didn't want him to realize Max considered him the prime suspect in the thefts.

"What'd you want to talk to me about, Miss Sheridan?" Amad asked as the other kids were filing out of the conference room. "I can't stay but a minute. I promised Mr. Twilling—my supervisor," he elaborated at her blank look, "that I wouldn't be late. He's got a department head meeting to go to, and the other person on the floor called in sick, so you see he's depending on me." Amad's face glowed with youthful pride, and Kiley felt sick. If she couldn't figure out how to clear him . . .

Determinedly, she pushed her fears aside. "Amad, do you remember earlier in the week when that electronic timer disappeared out of the display case in your department?"

"Mr. Winthrop told you about that, huh?" Amad looked regretful, but not guilty, she was relieved to see.

"He did mention it, and I was curious," Kiley probed.

"I don't really know a lot about it," Amad said. "Mr. Twilling thinks that it happened while he was at that meeting, but I don't, and neither does David."

"David?" Kiley asked.

"Yeah, he dropped by to talk to me on his way back from his break."

"And David saw the timer in the case?"

"No, but he was standing there with me for almost ten minutes until I got busy and he left."

"Did you tell Mr. Winthrop that David was there?" Kiley asked.

"Course not! What do you think I am? A fink?" Amad looked outraged.

"No, but—"

"David wasn't supposed to be there talking to me. If I told, he'd get in trouble, and he doesn't know anything about the timer. I asked him first thing the next morning. I won't do nothin' to get my friends in trouble."

"No, of course not," Kiley said soothingly. "I was just curious. I'm sure David's very nice."

"He is," Amad said emphatically. "I'll see you, Miss Sheridan. I gotta go." He hurried out, closing the door behind him with a gentle thump.

So David Mallings had been there, Kiley mused. David could have stolen the timer. But why would he? She frowned. If he wanted a timer, he could afford to buy one. Or, more accurately, his father could. On the surface it seemed highly unlikely that David would have taken either the timer or Priscilla. But, it was equally unlikely that he would befriend Amad.

Oh, hell! Kiley glared at the conference table. Maybe she was becoming a cynic. Maybe David was exactly what he appeared to be. A nice kid with a bright future who'd taken a liking to Amad. Amad was certainly likable enough. But Amad was also very vulnerable, and she had to find out for sure if David was what he seemed to be.

She paused while stuffing papers into her briefcase as she suddenly remembered Jane Anderson. On the day of the picnic she'd said that she listened to gossip but didn't embellish on it. Jane had been at the store for years. Maybe she would know more about David. Kiley checked the time. If she was quick about it, she should be able to catch Jane before she went to lunch.

To her relief, she found Jane in her office, frowning over a huge stack of computer printouts.

"Hi, Kiley. If you're looking for someone to eat with, you've come to the right place. I'm starved. Just give me five minutes to finish this page."

Kiley carefully closed the door to Jane's office and sat down. "Lunch sounds good, but before we go I'm hoping you can give me some information," she said slowly, trying to decide how to phrase her question.

"About our fearless leader?" Jane grinned at her. "I'd say you already know more than anyone in the store. At least more about the things that count."

Kiley felt a brief spurt of pleasure at Jane's words before she remembered that she also knew just how stubborn Max could be.

"It's not about Max, it's about David Mallings."

"David Mallings?" Jane frowned. "What do you want to know about him and why?"

"I'd rather not say why, and as to what . . . Well, do you know if there's anything in his background that is less than . . ." Kiley gestured impotently with her hand.

At Jane's puzzled look, Kiley realized that Jane took confidences very seriously. "It's very important for the future of one of my students and this program. Please."

Jane relented. "If you're asking my opinion and you understand that it's only my opinion and I don't want it repeated to anyone," she warned, and Kiley nodded. "I think David is a classic example of a kid born to a self-made father. Jim was raised in an orphanage, and from some of the things he's said, his childhood was pretty grim. He's determined that David is going to have everything he missed."

"With what result?"

"Primarily, that David not only doesn't have much of a sense of responsibility, but he is of the firm opinion that dear old Dad can fix everything. Like that incident right after he graduated from high school."

"What incident?"

"Oh, nothing terrible. It was just that he and a bunch of friends crashed a party some girl was giving while her parents were out of town, and they trashed the house. Literally."

"What happened?"

"The boys' fathers agreed to pay for all the damages and the girl's folks dropped the charges. But the point I'm making is that Jim took responsibility for the mess, and not David."

"I see." Kiley frowned thoughtfully. "What about since?"

"No trouble that I've heard of. He managed to get a college degree—barely. Amy over in personnel said that he'd never have been hired for our management training program if it hadn't been for his dad. We all think the world of Jim."

"Yes, he was very nice to Amad, one of my students," Kiley agreed.

Jane nodded. "The outgoing one. I met him the other day in the cafeteria. He's going to be a force to be reckoned with around here when he matures enough to learn how to use all that charm."

*If he lasts long enough*, Kiley thought with forboding. "Thanks for the information, Jane. How about if I go down to the cafeteria and save us a seat?"

"I'll be there in five minutes." Jane turned to her printout as Kiley left.

Walking down the hall, Kiley considered what she had learned. David had been involved in a stupid, destructive stunt while in high school, and his father had rescued him. He was a mediocre student who owed his job to his father's efforts and not his own. She grimaced. A similar charge could be leveled at Amad. He was a less-than-mediocre student, and he owed his job to her efforts.

But Amad had never trashed anyone's home. Or been in any kind of trouble with the police. Although the incident had happened four years ago, she reminded herself. A lifetime in terms of maturity to someone David's age. Not only that, but she had no way of knowing just how involved he'd been. He could have been no more than a member of the group who'd done the damage. He could have been guilty by association.

Kiley leaned against the wall as she waited for the elevator to arrive. That incident was only relevant in that it portrayed David as a spoiled young man. But being spoiled didn't necessarily translate into being a thief. She sighed in frustration.

The elevator arrived and Kiley stepped inside, trying not to feel discouraged that her first attempt at detective work had been singularly unsuccessful. Eventually she'd figure out some way to convince Max that Amad wasn't a thief. She pressed her lips together in determination. She'd make Max listen.

# 9

THE WORK WEEK ENDED with Kiley no closer to finding a solution to the thefts, but she consoled herself with the thought that nothing else in the store had disappeared. At least she didn't think so. Max hadn't referred to the subject again, and she was reluctant to bring it up. Talking about the thefts wasn't going to solve them. It merely caused friction between them, and she didn't want to do that. She didn't want to do anything to remind either of them that there were some treacherous undercurrents beneath the seemingly smooth surface of their developing relationship. She wasn't so naive as to think that ignoring the problem would make it go away, but ignoring it did allow her to concentrate on other things. Such as Max, and how he looked and felt, and more importantly, how he made her feel.

As she got ready for the party, Kiley decided to try her best to forget what had happened and concentrate on enjoying her evening with Max. And she would enjoy it, she vowed, stepping into her new dress with a feeling of excited anticipation. It was easily the most gorgeous dress she'd ever owned—as well as the sexiest. Made of a thin, textured jade silk, the crossover bodice fastened at the waist with two large buttons. The deeply cut neckline made wearing a bra impossible, and the feel of the sleek lining rubbing across her bare breasts added to her feeling of sensual awareness.

Kiley pirouetted in front of her bathroom mirror. She felt like a sexy, desirable woman capable of anything.

At the sound of her door chimes, she hurriedly jammed her feet into green strappy sandals and rushed to answer it, eager to see Max's reaction.

The expression in his eyes was all she could have hoped for, and she spent the short ride to his friends' home wrapped in a warm glow of contentment.

"Who all's going to be here?" Kiley asked Max as they approached their host's front door.

"Everyone," Max said dryly. "Marcia is very active in several charities, and the more people she entertains, the more sources she has when she wants something."

"Aha! You mean I'm not the only one who wants things."

"All Marcia ever wants is money. You demand personal involvement, and I've got my father as an example of what can result from that."

"Think of it as stars for your crown," Kiley suggested.

"What crown?"

"My grandmother used to tell me that every time you did a good deed, God put a star in your crown for heaven."

Max ran his finger over her soft cheek and smiled tenderly at her.

Kiley shivered at the eddies of excitement that swirled through her at his touch.

"If that's true, Kiley Sheridan, then you're never going to be able to hold your head up under the weight of all those stars."

"Thank you." She smiled, touched by his compliment. "I—" She turned as the door opened and a buxom woman in her early forties greeted them.

"Max, darling." The woman gave him a quick hug and a kiss on the cheek. "I'm so glad you were able to make it. And who's your friend?"

"Kiley Sheridan. Kiley, Marcia Tottenham."

"Hello, Kiley Sheridan." Kiley was briefly embraced in a fragrant cloud of perfume. "I just adore your dress. I wish I was thin enough to wear something like that." Marcia's sincerity was unmistakable, and Kiley felt herself warming to the woman. "Just go on in and help yourself to something to drink," she said as she turned to greet another set of arriving guests.

They had been there almost two hours when the four-piece orchestra, which had been playing soft music, gave an energetic imitation of a drumroll.

"All right, everyone." Marcia held up her hands for quiet. "Listen up. We have just arrived at the high point of the evening."

Kiley obediently tore her glassy-eyed gaze away from a middle-aged man named Warren who was regaling her with his latest coup in the stock market and turned toward her hostess.

"We . . ." Marcia paused for dramatic effect then announced, "we are going to have a treasure hunt."

A treasure hunt? Kiley frowned. She hadn't been on a treasure hunt since she was a Girl Scout.

"And the prize for the winning couple will be a pair of tickets to next week's performance of *Pagliacci* at Wolf Trap."

"That's great," Warren enthused. "I tried to get tickets to that yesterday, and they were sold out. Trust Marcia to come up with some spares."

"Uh-huh," Kiley agreed, searching her memory in an attempt to remember exactly what *Pagliacci* was. "Isn't that an opera?" she finally asked.

"You could say that." He gave her a patronizing smile that raised her hackles.

"I just did say that," she said tartly.

"Could it be that you don't care for opera?" Warren stared at her in disbelief.

"Sure could," she said cheerfully.

"There you are, Kiley. I've been looking all over for you." Max's deep voice slipped over her, heightening her awareness of the things around her. "Evening, Warren."

"I might have known she was with you when she said she didn't like opera," Warren said in disgust.

"Ah, an intelligent woman." Max gave her an approving smile.

"You two are a pair of philistines," Warren grumbled.

"If each of you will choose your partners," Marcia continued, "you may pick up your first clue from me. And let me tell you right now that everyone will eventually get the same set of clues. They are simply staggered so you won't all be in the same place at the same time."

"Kiley, would you—" Warren began.

"No, she wouldn't," Max said. "Go find your own date. Kiley's mine."

"Ah, well." Warren gave her a rueful grin. "I tried to save you, my dear."

"Just for that, if we win, we won't give you the tickets." Max looked down his nose at him.

"How about selling them to me?" Warren asked craftily.

"You're offering us money? Filthy lucre in the same breath as a cultural event like *Pagliacci*?" Max gave Warren a look of mock horror. "Speaking of philistines . . ."

"Don't mind him, Warren," Kiley told the frustrated-looking little man. "If by some freak chance we should win, you can have mine."

"Thank you, dear lady." He beamed at her. "In that case you'd better get started while I try to find a partner." He motioned them toward their hostess.

"You should have held out for cold, hard cash." Max picked up a slip of paper form the table beside Marcia and shepherded Kiley out of the way of the milling couples.

She chuckled. "I'm not a complete philistine."

"Take my word for it, philistines have a lot more fun." He unfolded the strip of paper and stared at it.

"Why a treasure hunt?" Kiley asked, surreptitiously studying the other couples who were reading their clues.

"Because Marcia is a mystery fan, and for fan read fanatic. Her idea of a perfect weekend is a mystery lovers' getaway weekend where everyone spends time trying to solve a murder."

"Let me see our clue." Kiley looked at it. "Good Lord, it says this is the first of twenty clues! She must have done an incredible amount of work on these."

"Marcia is tireless in her pursuit of a mystery."

"To say nothing of inscrutable. Listen to this. 'On Pegasus's flying wings, *Pagliacci* hangs.'"

"*Pagliacci* can hang, period, for all I care," Max grumbled.

"On Pegasus's flying wings," Kiley said, musingly. "And we have to figure it out in order to get our next clue."

"Unfortunate but true. Would you like a drink?"

"No, I'd like some help. Pegasus. Hmm. Pegasus was a flying horse. So where would you go looking for a flying horse?"

"In a book of Greek mythology?"

"Sounds reasonable to me. Are there any books around?"

"In the library. We might as well look." He led her through the house to a large room near the front. The room's walls were lined with books, ranging from leather-bound classics to dog-eared paperbacks.

Kiley sighed as she glanced over the nearest shelf. "We can forget this idea. The books aren't alphabetized. It'd take all night to find anything in here. How about a book left lying on a table or a desk?" She glanced around the room, but there was no seemingly carelessly placed book in plain sight. "Hmm, I think we've drawn a blank on this idea."

"Suppose Pegasus was real," Max said slowly. "Where would you expect to find him?"

"Greece?"

"Not even Marcia would go to those extremes."

"Well then, if I had a horse, flying or otherwise, I'd put him in the stables."

"Sounds reasonable. Let's go look." Max took her arm and headed through the house.

"Look where?"

"In the stables." He guided her through the conferring couples on the patio and onto a softly lit pathway through the shrubbery.

"Of course, why didn't I think of that?" she said ruefully, for a moment feeling entirely out of her element. The people she knew had garages in their backyards, not stables.

"Because men are naturally smarter?" His teeth gleamed whitely in the dim light.

"I don't know about smarter, but you're sure as heck a lot braver if you've got the nerve to make an idiotic comment like that around an able-bodied woman."

"Is your body able?" Max's smile widened, and Kiley felt a shaft of excitement pierce her.

"The question isn't whether it's able, but whether it's willing," she said repressively.

"Would it help if I said I was willing?"

"You don't have to tell me that. You already said it all when you said you were a man."

"Talk about stereotyping . . ."

"Let's not," she said. The problem was that Max's teasing had tapped into her own longings, and she couldn't respond with the degree of lightheartedness that was called for.

"Is that the stable?" She pointed to a small barnlike building to their right.

"Uh-huh." Max looked around. Except for a couple farther down the pathway and someone or something crashing around in the bushes, the area was deserted. "Come on. Let's take a look while we've still got it to ourselves."

Kiley walked into the barn, being careful where she stepped, while Max found the lights and switched them on. A closer inspection proved her fears groundless. The floor was spotless. It was also bare of anything that even vaguely looked like their next clue. "I guess I was wrong," she said.

Max rubbed his jaw thoughtfully. "Not necessarily. Remember, the clue said Pegasus."

"So?"

"Pegasus spent a lot of time in the air." He stared thoughtfully at the ceiling high above.

Kiley followed his glance, but saw nothing unusual. "Tell me, was he invisible, too?"

Max ignored the question. "How about the loft? It's up in the air, relatively speaking."

"This whole thing is up in the air," she said in resignation. "Is there a loft?"

"Has to be. Where else would you store the hay?" He headed toward the back of the stables.

"First of all, I don't see any horses, and second, even if I did, I still wouldn't know." She followed him into the gloom. "I've never been on a horse in my life."

"You haven't missed a thing. Horses are overgrown, smelly brutes with uncertain dispositions, and that's on their good days. Aha!" He pointed triumphantly toward an open staircase against the back wall. "Our way up."

"I'd rather have a way out," she grumbled as she started up the stairs.

The loft was inadequately lit by one overhead light, and Kiley stopped at the head of the stairs and peered around. Seeing nothing, she started across the floor, carefully weaving her way around the shoulder-high stacks of baled hay.

She yelped and jumped back as a swaying white apparition suddenly appeared to her left.

Caught off guard, Max stumbled. His arms automatically closed around her as he fell, cradling her against his chest. The hard planes of his body pushed into her much softer flesh, and she unconsciously wiggled, trying to find a more comfortable spot. There was nothing the least bit comfortable in her present position. It made her feel distinctly unsettled.

Kiley licked her dry lips as she felt his body hardening beneath her. She closed her eyes helplessly as the heat and scent of his vividly masculine body overwhelmed her. The musky aroma of the hay added an earthy scent, which somehow was in keeping with the increasingly primitive cast of her feelings.

"I, uh, I'm sorry I tripped you," she offered into the tension-filled air. "I saw something white and I—"

Max turned his head and looked. "The missing clue, no doubt," he said dispassionately. At the moment all that interested him was the fact that he finally had Kiley where he wanted her. In his arms.

Now what, she asked herself. If she stayed sprawled on top of Max, she was as good as telling him that she liked the position. But, her mind countered, since he wasn't trying to stand up, he must like it, too.

"What are you thinking?" Max's voice sounded husky in the dim light.

"How good you feel," she replied honestly.

"Me?" Max's chuckle shook his chest, pressing it into her breasts. "Darling, you have a corner on the feeling-good market." His voice deepened perceptibly as his hands closed over her soft hips, holding them tightly against his hard thighs.

Tremors chased over her skin and she moved sensuously against his hardness. His response was instantaneous. His hand closed around the back of her head and pulled her down so that his lips could capture hers.

He rolled onto his side, still holding her locked against him as he deepened the kiss. Kiley arched into him, incapable of rational thought. She felt his fingers fumbling with the buttons that held the front of her dress together, then the warm night air rushed over her suddenly bare skin.

Max rolled her onto her back in the thick straw, and his hands covered her breasts.

Kiley gasped as sharp fragments of desire sliced through her. He drank the sound from her lips and began to slowly rub his thumbs over the soft pink tips, convulsing them into tight buds.

"Do you like that?" he murmured. "I do. You feel so good beneath my hands." He bent his head and Kiley tensed as she felt his warm breath on her sensitive skin. When his tongue rasped over her nipples, a tormented groan came out of her throat, and she clutched his shoulders, her nails digging into his suit jacket. Her hands slipped inside the jacket to pluck ineffectively at his shirt. She wanted to feel his skin against hers.

"Yes. Most definitely yes," Kiley muttered roughly, pulling his shirt out of his pants and deftly unbuttoning it. Supporting his weight on his arms, he slowly lowered himself onto her straining breasts until the tips were buried in the thick mat of hair that covered his chest. Methodically, he began to rub back and forth. The abrasive movement sent waves of longing through her, and she whimpered as her breasts hardened with the need for his touch.

"God, you're exquisite," he whispered as he studied her rapt expression. Lowering his head, he took the tip of one breast in his mouth and sucked strongly on it.

Kiley reached for him, but to her dismay he suddenly lifted his head.

"Max, please." Her voice was liquid with her need.

"Shh." He dropped a hard, frustrated kiss on her parted lips. "Listen." He hurriedly got to his feet and half carried, half dragged her to the back of the loft, where he pulled her behind a stack of hay bales.

"Let me guess," she whispered. "This treasure hunt has a spy element?"

"Shh." He put his arm around her shoulder and pulled her against him. Her cheek was pressed against his chest and a dreamy smile curved her lips at the heated texture of his skin. She kissed him then began to tug at the crisp cloud of hair with her lips, discovering his flat nipples underneath. Wondering if his were as sensitive as hers, she lightly caressed the pebbly hard point with the tip of her tongue. The shudder that shook him gave her her answer, and a feeling of power surged through her.

The sudden sound of high heels on the bare wooden steps interrupted her absorption and she frowned in annoyance, realizing why Max had so summarily rushed her to the back of the loft. Someone else was in the barn following the same clue.

"I'm not going into those bales of hay," Kiley heard a feminine voice proclaim. "I tell you I heard something scrambling around up here. It's probably full of mice. Or worse."

"I think she's referring to you," Kiley whispered to Max.

"Oh, all right, stay there for all I care," a male voice said in disgust. "I'll look around." His voice came closer. "There're the clues. Hanging from the ceiling."

"Well, grab one and let's get out of here," the woman said. "This place gives me the creeps. I feel like something's watching me."

"If you'd lay off reading Stephen King, you'd— Say. . ." The man's voice was thoughtful. "Is anyone downstairs?"

"Not that I can see. Or hear, for that matter. Why?"

"We could take all the clues, and that would slow everyone else down."

"That doesn't seem very sporting."

"You know what they say," the man began.

"Cheaters never prosper," Kiley moaned in a hoarse whisper.

The effect was electrifying. The woman let out a scream that raised the hairs on the back of Kiley's neck and took off down the stairs at breakneck speed.

"Lindsay, come back here," the man yelled. "That's no ghost. It's—"

"The witness to a dastardly deed," Max intoned pontifically from behind the bales.

"I recognize your voice, Max Winthrop, and I'll get you for this. Just you wait." The man hurried down the stairs after the still-shrieking Lindsay.

"Come on. Let's make our escape while the coast is clear." Max hauled Kiley to her feet and hastily buttoned his shirt while she fastened her dress. "Lindsay's caterwauling will bring them all down on us."

"It was worth it." Kiley chuckled as she brushed bits of straw off her dress. "Of all the underhanded tricks he was going to pull... Hey, you forgot to get the clue," she told him as he started hustling her toward the stairs.

"I already found the treasure. Let's go back to the house. I need a good stiff drink."

Or a cold shower, Kiley thought ruefully as she followed him, picking hay out of her hair as she went.

They were rounding the swimming pool beside the patio when a gigantic sneeze shook her.

"Gesundheit," Max said.

"Thank you. I—" Kiley was engulfed in another series of sneezes.

"What's wrong?" Max eyed her worriedly.

"Oh, dear." Kiley sneezed again then sniffed as her nose begin to drip.

"Here." Max shoved a snowy white handkerchief at her. "An allergy?" he guessed.

"Uh-huh." She sniffed into his hanky. "There must have been mold in that hay." She picked a piece off her dress and peered closely at it.

"If there is, then you must be covered with it."

"Probably." She sneezed again.

Max took her arm and hustled her through the house.

"What's the rush?" she protested as she hurried to keep up with him.

"You need to wash the mold off you before something serious happens."

Kiley sniffed. "It doesn't get any worse than this. I have allergies, not asthma. But I do want to wash it off. The sneezing's bad enough, but I'm starting to itch."

"Kiley! What's wrong?" Marcia caught up with them on the front steps. "Warren saw you sneezing your head off. Are you all right?"

"Not to worry," Kiley said soothingly. "I just ran afoul of some mold in the barn loft."

"You poor dear," Marcia sympathized.

"And she needs to wash it off," Max said.

"Of course she does," Marcia agreed as Max bundled Kiley into his car. "I'm sorry the evening ended so abruptly for you," she continued. "You must come again. Some time when we can have a good long talk."

"Thank you, Marcia. I'd like to," Kiley called as Max accelerated down the driveway.

"Blast Marcia and her mysteries," Max muttered as Kiley sneezed again.

"It's not poor Marcia's fault that I forgot about my allergy," Kiley said fairly, "and once I get home and shower, it'll stop."

"We'll go to my place. It's only five minutes away. If that's okay?" Max shot her a quick, penetrating look, and Kiley felt a surge of heat warm her skin at the expression in his eyes. There was more to his question than where she took a shower. A lot more.

Kiley glanced at her hands and tried to think, but the problem was she didn't want to think. All she wanted to do was to feel. If she started to think, she'd start to worry about Amad and the future. Tonight was an island in time, she told herself. Divorced from the problems of the past and future. It was as if she and Max inhabited a magic territory that nothing could enter. As long as they stayed within it, they were safe.

She took a deep breath and said, "I'd like that very much, Max."

"You won't regret it. I'll take care of everything."

"Thank you," Kiley murmured, having no fears on that score. Max was a responsible man who wouldn't expose her to any unnecessary risks.

A sense of rightness engulfed her as she followed Max into the house.

"Into the shower with you, and the sooner the better," he said. "Use my bedroom. It's the room at the end of the hall on the right. I'll use the shower down here."

"But . . ." Her objection was swallowed in a sneeze.

"I was in that hay, too, remember? I don't want you to sneeze every time I come near."

"No, I guess not." Kiley gave him a rueful smile.

"Up you go, darling." Max put his hands on her shoulders and gently pushed her toward the stairs. "I'll join you shortly."

Kiley went, her rising sense of excitement only partially dimmed by the sneezes that continued to rack her. She found Max's bedroom easily enough and hurried across the beautiful cream and gold Aubusson carpet toward a door that led to the bathroom. She glanced around the voluptuous splendor in delight, a delight that faded as she caught sight of herself in the ceiling-to-floor plate glass mirror lining one of the bathroom walls.

Her eyes were beginning to swell and her nose was bright red, but nothing could diminish the brilliant sparkle of anticipation darkening her eyes to bitter chocolate. Kiley felt as if she was teetering on the brink of a momentous discovery. A discovery that would broaden and deepen and enrich her life more than anything she'd ever known.

And it all revolved around Max, she thought dreamily. Her whole world had narrowed to Max. Her moment of introspection was broken as she noticed the bits of straw in her hair. She'd have to shampoo it, she decided. She had no intention of prolonging this infernal sneezing any longer than she had to.

Hurriedly stripping off her clothes, Kiley made short work of washing away the mold in the shower. Ten minutes later, she wrapped her dripping hair in a towel, dried off her body and looked around for something to wear.

Her new dress was out of the question. It would need to be dry-cleaned before she could wear it again. She opened the linen closet in search of a dry towel to wrap around herself and found a white terry bathrobe hanging on the back of the door.

With a pleased murmur, she slipped into it, tied the belt around her narrow waist, took a deep, steadying breath and went in search of Max.

She found him in the bedroom. He was sitting in one of the overstuffed chairs in front of the fireplace wearing a robe similar to hers and holding a glass containing an inch of amber liquid.

"Come sit down and I'll dry your hair for you."

Slowly, Kiley crossed the large room, trying to control the excitement that threatened to suffocate her—an excitement she could see reflected in the glitter in Max's eyes.

He set his drink on the table beside him, and Kiley gracefully sank on the floor in front of him. As he shifted slightly to draw her between his legs, his robe partially opened, and Kiley could see the dark hair that liberally covered his powerful thighs.

She licked her dry lips, wanting nothing so much as to press them against his firm skin. To savor the taste and texture of it.

Max began to briskly rub her hair with the thick towel. She could feel his fingertips pressing against her scalp, and it sent a tingle of awareness ricocheting through her.

"There." After what seemed like an age to her beleaguered senses, Max tossed the towel on the carpet and ran his fingers through her damp hair. "I think that took care of the worst of it."

Kiley searched for something to say and came up with an anemic sounding, "That's nice."

"Would you like a drink?" He offered her his glass.

She took it and sniffed the contents. "Brandy?" she guessed.

"Uh-huh."

Kiley took a sip, her eyes watering as the liquor hit the back of her throat. "Thank you," she breathed hoarsely.

Max took the glass from her, set it on the table then swept her in his arms and started toward his king-size bed.

Kiley snuggled happily against his chest.

He gently placed her on the bed then stood beside her watching her with hot, devouring eyes. As if he found her body as engrossing as she found his. The knowledge gave her confidence. Reaching for him, she rubbed her palm along his jawline, delighting in the abrasive texture of his skin. She felt as if she could spend the rest of her life exploring his body and it would never lose its fascination for her.

Max shrugged out of his robe, opened the drawer in the bedside table and took out a small foil packet.

Kiley's eyes slipped over his broad chest, following the way his hair arrowed down to his flat abdomen. Her breath left her body in a rush at the sight of his fully aroused manhood.

Slowly sinking down on the bed beside her, deliberately prolonging the moment, Max unfastened the belt on her robe and pushed the edges apart as if he was unwrapping a package of inestimable worth. His features had hardened, and her heart raced at the expression in his eyes.

"My beautiful Kiley," Max crooned. He molded his hands over her breasts, and she gasped, pushing upward in an attempt to intensify the sensation of his palm scraping over her soft, sensitive skin. She felt as if she was going to explode with the force of the feeling rioting through her.

His expression totally absorbed, Max began to trace ever widening circles around her breasts.

Kiley gasped as the sparks pouring off his questing fingertips penetrated her skin, setting off a quivering deep inside her. Hungrily, she stared at his mouth, her eyes longingly tracing its contours. She wanted to feel those lips against hers, to taste him. Wanted it with a longing that was swamping all other considerations.

Sensing her need, Max touched her mouth with his, parting her lips to allow his tongue entrance. Slowly, with a methodical thoroughness that sent her heartbeat into overdrive, Max explored the shape of her mouth. His brandy-flavored breath combined with his skillful tongue to set all her pulse points pounding in unison. She could hear the primitive rhythm of her heartbeat echoing in her ears, adding to her sense of abandonment. Her emotions seemed to be spinning out of control, and she gasped his name in an agony of longing.

Responding, Max nudged her legs apart with his knee and positioned himself between them, his heated hardness pressing against her.

She arched her body invitingly, frantic to feel him within her. A part of her.

Max slowly pressed forward, the hot, blunt length of him filling her, and she shuddered as she struggled to accept him.

He scraped his tongue over the tip of one of her breasts and a small whimper escaped her. She could feel a tremendous pressure building within her. A pressure that threatened to consume her, and she didn't want that to happen. Not yet. She wanted this incredible experience to last and last, but she knew it wouldn't. It couldn't. She could feel the tension fast approaching the breaking point.

Max's mouth closed over her breast as he began to move with swift, powerful strokes.

Kiley clutched his shoulders and let his movements carry her out of herself into a world of pure sensation where anything was possible. Dimly, as if from a great distance she heard Max's shout of satisfaction, then he collapsed on top of her, his large body seemingly boneless. Lovingly, she cradled him, reveling in the feel of his heavy weight trapping her against the bed. She felt bereft when he rolled onto his side, even though he still held her tightly against his chest.

"I'll squash you," he answered her muttered protest.

"But what a way to go," Kiley answered dreamily.

Max chuckled. "It might be worth it at that. We'll discuss variations when we've both recovered."

# 10

KILEY MUTTERED IN PROTEST as a brilliant ray of sun-shine burned across her face, nudging her awake. Groggily, she turned her head away from the irritation and opened her eyes, then opened them wider when she saw Max's sleep-relaxed face on the pillow beside her.

Her mind snapped to instant awareness as her memory came flooding back. Wonderingly, she stared at Max as if she'd never seen him before. His ebony hair was tousled against the snowy white pillowcase, and her fingertips tingled as she remembered its silky texture. His thick eyelashes made a dark fan against his tanned skin, and his cheeks were covered with a blueish-black shadow that made her long to explore its texture. He looked younger in sleep. Younger and more relaxed. As if what had happened last night had rejuvenated him.

As it had her. Kiley stretched voluptuously, relishing the feel of the sleek percale sheets against her bare skin. She felt fantastic. An ecstatic smile curved her lips. Absolutely fantastic. As if she'd suddenly discovered the secret of life. Last night had been a revelation to her in more ways than one. It was as if she and Max really had discovered a magical oasis where the tensions and problems that seemed to constantly swirl around her students couldn't touch them.

She knew it couldn't last, but while it did she intended to cherish every moment. Starting now. She slowly leaned toward Max, intending to wake him with a kiss, but before she could reach him the phone rang.

Max's eyes flew open at the intrusive noise, and a slow smile curved his lips as he saw her.

"Good morning, Kiley. I—" He frowned as the phone rang again. Twisting around, he picked up the bedside clock and stared at it in disbelief.

"It can't be twelve-twenty," Kiley protested.

"Well, we didn't actually fall asleep until almost dawn." Max's eyes burned hotly with remembered pleasure. "We—" The phone rang again.

"Oh, for—" Max reached for it with one hand and with the other pulled Kiley's unresisting body against his sleep-warmed limbs.

Contented by his actions, Kiley snuggled closer and began to nuzzle the skin at the base of his neck, exploring the pattern of his emerging beard. She had reached his earlobe when his unnatural tenseness finally penetrated her self-absorption.

She tilted her head and peered into his face. The lazy good humor of a moment ago was gone, replaced by anger.

Kiley waited until he hung up, then asked, "What's wrong?"

Max eyed her thoughtfully and Kiley felt a shiver of fear as she stared into his narrowed eyes.

Max had changed. That phone call had jolted him out of the role of indulgent lover and into...what? She scrambled to her knees, hugging the sheet around her.

"What's wrong, Max?" she repeated apprehensively.

Max hesitated. He didn't want to tell her that yet another expensive item was missing from a place Amad had access to. He didn't want to see her eyes darken with pain. He wanted them to be warm and glowing with pleasure in the aftermath of their lovemaking. He wanted to take her in his arms and make love to her until she forgot everything but him and the incredible emotions they shared. But he couldn't lie to her. What they shared was much too precious to be contaminated with lies, no matter how well intended.

He sighed. "That was Don Acton."

"Acton?" Kiley tried to place the name and failed.

"He's in charge of security. I asked him to call me if anything disappeared from an area where Amad has been."

"You discussed your ridiculous suspicions about Amad with someone else?" Kiley demanded.

"Not with someone else," Max said patiently. "With the head of security. It's his job."

"What is? To railroad Amad into jail? So what is he supposed to have taken this time?"

"A Rolex watch is missing from the jewelry department. It was there when the department head sold a similar one yesterday afternoon and was gone when she came in to work today."

"Amad doesn't work in jewelry," Kiley pointed out.

"No, but he visits a friend there on his way to breaks and at lunchtime."

Kiley opened her mouth then closed it as something suddenly occurred to her. "Let me guess. Jewelry is where David Mallings is assigned."

"Well, yes, but—"

"Max." Kiley's voice shook with the effort it took her to remain calm. "Everything you've said about Amad is equally true for David. He visits Amad in sporting goods, too."

"But why would David steal anything? Jim has—"

"We aren't talking about his father. We're talking about David."

"Kiley," Max said, "you can't clear Amad by pinning the blame on David."

"And you can't make Amad guilty simply because the kid was misguided enough to admire your silver." Kiley's voice rose in frustration.

"There's a whole lot more to this than my silver."

"Circumstantial evidence, all of it," Kiley clipped out. "There's not a shred of real proof anywhere."

"Acton's working on it," Max said, and Kiley felt a chill race over her skin. Everyone was working against Amad.

"I won't let you do this to Amad," Kiley vowed. "He didn't steal anything, and somehow I'll prove it." Swallowing the angry, frustrated tears that clogged the back of her throat, she climbed out of bed and looked around for the robe she'd so blissfully discarded last night. Last night and what they'd shared seemed a life-time away.

"Kiley." Max reached for her, but she danced out of his way. Their magical territory had been breached, and the real world had flowed in with a vengeance, she thought grimly.

"I want to go home, and I'd appreciate it if you'd loan me a shirt and a pair of shorts so I don't have to put my dress on until I can get it cleaned," she said with a dig-nity that wasn't at all impaired by the sheet she was clutching around herself.

Max sighed, realizing this wasn't the time to try to reason with her. She was much too upset. He'd do bet-ter to give her a chance to cool off. "My dressing room is through there." He nodded toward the door beside the bathroom. "Help yourself."

"Thank you," she muttered, and beat a hasty re-treat.

KILEY WASN'T SURE whether she was relieved when Max acceded to her demand without an argument and drove her home. One part of her wanted him to take her in his arms and smother all her doubts and fears under a bar-rage of kisses. But she knew, deep in her heart, that she could no longer go on pretending that everything was fine. She'd already tried that, and look what had hap-pened. The situation had erupted when she'd least expected it to. At the precise moment when she was the most vulnerable.

It all seemed so unfair, she thought drearily as she let herself into her house. To have found what she had with Max and then to have everything spoiled by something outside their control... She sniffed disconsolately.

But what did she have with Max, she asked herself as she sank down on her couch and tried to think. She needed to logically analyze what seemed to vibrate between them. The problem was that her feelings for Max weren't the least bit logical. They were a jumbled mass of emotions ranging from a deep respect for his intellect and his bone-deep sense of integrity to a primitive lust for his magnificent body.

"You're in love with the man." Her hushed whisper echoed around her living room with the impact of a gunshot. "You're in love with Max Winthrop," she repeated more firmly.

A sense of peace engulfed her. Of course she was in love with him. It had been inevitable from the moment she'd met him. He was everything she'd ever wanted in a man, and a whole lot more.

The sense of rightness that filled her was quickly superceded by hopelessness. How could their relationship grow with all the external pressures battering it? She took a deep, steadying breath. She didn't know, but she certainly intended to try. Try with all her heart. Somehow, she had to convince Max that he was wrong about Amad. But how? Her attempts to date had been singularly unsuccessful, which was hardly surprising, considering the fact that her detective skills had been garnered from reading a few Agatha Christie novels.

Kiley grimaced. It was all so frustrating when everything should have been perfect. Not only had she fallen deeply in love with a man who deserved her love, but she was also finally realizing her long-held dream of placing some of her students into good jobs with real futures. But the whole thing was flawed. Flawed by a situation she seemed helpless to change. But if she wasn't having any luck changing it, maybe she could outlast it, she thought. Time should be on her side. Max had said he wouldn't act without proof, and since Amad hadn't stolen anything, Acton wouldn't be able to find that proof. All she needed was the patience to hang in there and hope the real thief made a mistake and got caught.

But by Tuesday she was beginning to think that it wasn't patience she needed. It was a miracle.

To her dismay, Max hadn't sought her out on Monday and she had had too much pride to go looking for him—at least without an impeccable excuse. Fortunately for her peace of mind, Wayland provided her with one Tuesday morning.

He burst into her office and blurted out, "I'm sorry, Miss Sheridan, but this job su—I mean . . ."

"Never mind, Wayland, I get your meaning. For heaven's sake sit down." She gestured toward the seat beside her desk. Kiley was not surprised by his comments. Wayland was having a lot of problems fitting into Winthrops.

Wayland gingerly sat down, eyed her warily for a few seconds then blurted out, "Are you mad?"

"No," she said honestly. "Disappointed that things aren't working out for you, but I'm not as naive as to believe that everyone is going to like retailing. The question is, where do we go from here?"

"Well, remember what they said on TV?"

"What?" Kiley asked cautiously.

"You know. About being all you can be."

"You mean the army?"

"That's right. I talked it over with my dad, and he thought it was a good idea, so last night we went down to see the recruiter."

"And?"

"And they're going to take me. I'm supposed to report for basic training in six weeks."

"Congratulations!" Kiley smiled at him.

"You really mean that?" Wayland looked worried.

"Sincerely and absolutely. It's a great idea. You'll not only get to travel, but it's a chance to learn a skill."

"That's what Dad said. I signed up to train in heating and cooling. He says that people may cut out a lot of things but heating's here to stay."

"Your dad's right. He must be very proud of you."

"Yeah, well . . ." Wayland ducked his head self-consciously. "You know what dads are, and mine's better than most."

"Then all that remains is for you to sever your connection with Winthrops in a professional manner."

"You mean I should tell them I quit?"

"Yes." Kiley nodded solemnly.

"My dad said I was to give two weeks' notice."

"Good advice." Kiley nodded. "Come on. I'll walk you over to personnel and get the ball rolling."

"Thanks, Miss Sheridan." Wayland followed her out the door. "All those papers they're forever wanting you to fill out . . . It's enough to give a body hives."

"It won't be so bad," Kiley said soothingly.

To Wayland's obvious relief, it wasn't. He merely had to sign several forms, then listen while they explained his options regarding his insurance coverage. Kiley left him waiting for the secretary to make his copy of his resignation form and went to find Max.

Aggie's office was deserted, but Max's door was ajar. Cautiously, Kiley stuck her head around it. Her heart seemed to swell with the strength of her feelings as she saw him sitting behind his desk. Lovingly, she watched as he ran his fingers through his thick hair, and her hands clenched under the force of her desire to do the same. To feel the soft, silky strands beneath her caressing fingers again.

Max looked up and saw her, and a surge of pleasure shot through him. He'd spent most of yesterday trying to figure out a neutral subject to use as an excuse to approach her. He felt if he could just get close enough to her he could break down the barrier she'd erected after that damnably ill-timed phone call from Acton. And once he broke down the barrier he intended to bind her to him so closely that when she found out the truth about Amad it wouldn't make any difference to their relationship.

Harry had dropped off a set of Christmas drawings Chris had done, providing him with an excuse to call her. And just as he'd been about to do so, here she was. It was as if he'd conjured her up out of the depths of his own longings.

Kiley unconsciously began to relax. Max really was glad to see her. His pleasure was unmistakable. It lit his eyes from within, giving them a warm glow.

"You must be psychic, Kiley. I was just about to call you. Take a look at these." He handed her a stack of thick cardboard squares. Mounted on each was a watercolor depicting various woodland animals, each engaged in a holiday activity. A smile curved her lips at the sight of a family of chipmunks decorating a Christmas tree.

"Oh, Max, the mice are precious." She pointed to a mother mouse baking cookies with her two children. "And best of all, there's no Santa Claus."

"Good lord, woman. What are you? Some kind of subversive? How can anyone not like Santa Claus?"

"Because he's the most unkind thing Madison Avenue ever foisted off on the American public."

"Oh, come on."

"I'm serious. Think about it a minute. Our culture says that if you're good, Santa will bring you lots of toys."

"So? What's wrong with that?"

"Nothing, for the majority of kids, but what about the ones whose parents are out of work or on welfare or barely make enough to pay the bills without extras like toys? What about them? Those poor little devils go to bed on Christmas Eve expecting Santa Claus to bring them gifts because they were good and what do they get? Nothing, but heartache, because it isn't how good you are that counts, it's how much money your folks have to spend."

"But there're lots of organizations that give out gifts—"

"Sure, days before Christmas for the newspapers to take pictures, so that the organization can go around wrapped in a glow of moral rectitude for bringing a spot of brightness to all those drab, wretched little lives," Kiley said scathingly.

"That's not only unfair, but it's a gross oversimplification," Max insisted. "Most of the organizations are motivated by a sincere desire to make sure no kid is left out at Christmas. By publicizing their efforts, they make even more people aware of the scope of the problem."

Kiley grimaced. "I know, I know. It's just so frustrating that so many people get hurt despite good intentions. Do you have any idea what those kids' parents must go through knowing they can't give their children what every other kid seems to be getting?"

"Some of the parents," Max insisted. "Some don't give a damn."

"They're a distinct minority. I'm sorry." She shrugged. "I know that people mean well and I know that a present a week before Christmas is a whole lot better than nothing and I also know that nothing's going to change."

"How would you change it, if you could?"

"Give the kids' presents to their parents so they could give them to their children on Christmas Day," she said promptly. "And, yes, I know it's an impractical idea," she said, anticipating his objection.

"On a large scale, yes," Max said, moving quickly to take advantage of anything that would tie her more closely to both him and events at the store. "But if you were willing to organize and coordinate it, we might have a go at changing our own small corner of the world next Christmas."

"How?" Kiley asked, rather surprised at his response.

"The store's employees normally exchange presents at our Christmas party. We could ask them to buy something for a child instead."

"Would they?"

"I think so. Most people want to help, they just don't see how they can make a difference. We'll show them. We can ask the ministers of several of Washington's poorer churches to give us the names of some of their parishioners' kids whose parents can't afford to buy them presents. We'll put their age, sex and present preference on the bulletin board in the employee lounge. Then anyone who wants to can adopt a child for Christmas."

"Why limit it just to employees?" Kiley said slowly. "You know that huge tree you always decorate on the main floor every year?"

"Uh-huh." Max nodded encouragingly.

"Well, this year why not cover it with numbered pink and blue bulbs? We could have the kids' names on a file in my office and just put their age, sex and gift preference on a bulb. We'd use pink ornaments for girls and blue for boys. The customers would pick one and we'd record the customer's name and the number of the kid they picked. Then," Kiley continued, growing more excited, "we'd replace the bulb with one of the antique decorations you normally use. The goal would be to replace all the colored bulbs with decorations."

"And when the customers buy something, they could turn it into the business offices." Max quickly picked up on her idea. "The store could wrap the gifts and send them out with the regular deliveries. No one, not even the recipient's neighbors, would know that they were donations. I think you've got something there," Max said thoughtfully. "We can do it in the suburban stores, too, but you'll need to get started right away. Something of that scope is going to take a lot of organizing."

"You mean it, Max?" Kiley asked.

"Of course, I mean it. I think it's a great idea. I'll give it the store's wholehearted support, and in exchange you quit bad-mouthing Santa, okay?"

"For you, anything." Kiley was hit with such a surge of love for him that it was all she could do to keep from blurting it out. But she didn't dare. There were enough external strains on their relationship without adding an internal one. Love could be a tremendous burden when it wasn't shared. And his feelings might not have grown with the same speed hers had. They might need a little longer to mature. But they would, she assured herself, refusing to consider the alternative.

"Now that has possibilities." Max's eyes took on a sudden gleam that made her stomach clench with excitement. "We could—" He broke off as the sound of Aggie returning to the outer office was clearly audible through the half-open door. "Dammit!" he swore in frustration. "We need a lock."

"If you put a lock on that door everyone will be wondering what you're up to."

"I'm up to anything you are, darling." Max gave her a lighthearted leer.

Kiley forced herself to remember where they were and said, "You never did tell me what those precious little animal watercolors were for."

"Chris did them. Harry had submitted some futuristic designs for the store windows for Christmas, and I sent them back. So he had Chris try his hand at it, and this is the result."

"Can you construct those kinds of scenes in the windows?"

"Sure. We'll order the animals and most of the accessories from a company that specializes in window displays. In fact—" Max glanced down to hide his excitement "—if I remember correctly we had animal displays in the windows at Christmas when I was just a kid. I remember watching a squirrel family riding around in an electric trolley."

He rubbed his jaw thoughtfully, and Kiley watched in mesmerized fascination as his hand moved across his supple skin.

"I wonder what ever became of them. Maybe Art remembers," he said, knowing full well where they were stored, but not wanting to be obvious about his desire to get her alone, away from interruptions.

He picked up the phone and punched in a few numbers.

Kiley let the husky sounds of Max's voice flow soothingly through her mind. Her attention was caught and held by the forceful movements of his hand as he made some point to the unseen Art. He had such strong hands, she thought. A slow, burning warmth began to heat her skin at the memory of those hands on her body, stroking, enticing . . .

"You never did tell me what you came to see me about." Max's voice intruded on her daydreams.

Kiley dragged her mind back to the present. "Um, it's about Wayland. He says he hates retailing and he's joined the army."

Max considered her words for a few seconds then said, "Actually that's not a bad idea. Call catering and have them send up the fixings for a party for your students on his last day."

"All right," Kiley said, wondering if the celebration was for Wayland or because Max had managed to get rid of one of her students in such a painless manner.

She grimaced, wishing she could ask him to hire someone else to take Wayland's place, but as things stood now she doubted he would agree. And she didn't think it would be a good idea to cause any more problems until she had managed to solve the gigantic one she already had.

Max watched the expressive play of emotions across her face and wondered what could have caused the tension he saw reflected there. Certainly not his suggesting a party. Eager to remove the look, he asked, "What do you have scheduled after your tutoring session with the kids?"

"Nothing in particular. Why?"

"Because Art thinks those antique animals the store used to display are stored out at my house in the attic. You could come along and help me look, if you'd like."

"Oh, I'd like," Kiley said with absolute sincerity. She was eager for any opportunity to spend time with Max. Especially away from the store, which seemed to be a constant reminder of all their problems.

# 11

"As I LIVE AND BREATHE, it's Aladdin's cave." Kiley looked around in awe as she surveyed the incredible collection of boxes, trunks, old toys and furniture stacked waist high in Max's attic. "This is fantastic."

"This is what happens when you have a bunch of pack rats for ancestors." Max frowned as he looked around. "If those animal characters are up here, then they should be in boxes with the Winthrop logo."

"Big deal." Kiley peered at the boxes closest to her. "All the boxes up here seem to have the store's logo on them."

"So they do." Max ran impatient fingers through his hair, eager to find the animals so he could do what he really wanted to do—take Kiley into his arms and kiss her until she could think of nothing but him. "How about if we look for something that hasn't been moved for a while. They have to have been sitting here for nearly twenty-five years."

"How are we going to know how long they've been here?" Kiley asked, "Everything's immaculate."

"That's because the cleaning service goes over it every two weeks. A lot of this furniture is antique."

Kiley looked at a massive headboard decorated with intricately carved gargoyles, goblins and gremlins. She shuddered at the thought of having the hideous little things leering down at her while she slept.

"Some of it's quite valuable," Max continued. "It's been banished to the attic for some reason or another."

"I can relate to that," Kiley said with one last glance at the headboard.

"Why don't you start at that end?" Max pointed to his left. "And I'll start at the other end. Shout if you find anything."

Kiley bit back her disappointment at being separated from Max. She knew that this way they could search twice as fast, and the sooner they found the animals . . . A dreamy expression chased across her face. She knew she hadn't mistaken the hot, burning look of promise Max had given her as he had helped her out of the car.

Leaving Max engrossed in the train set he was happily pulling out of a box, she wandered to the other end of the attic, unable to decide where to start looking. It was like being let loose in a chocolate shop and being told to help yourself.

Curious, Kiley pulled off the protective covering thrown over a long lump and discovered an exquisite chaise longue.

"Shades of Mae West," she muttered, having no trouble visualizing the sex symbol reclining on the faded green-silk upholstery. Gently, she ran her fingertips over the smooth cherry frame, wondering why anyone would put such a beautiful thing in the attic.

From its position behind all the boxes, it must have been discarded a long time ago.

She sat on it, sinking into the thick down cushions.

"Have you found anything yet?" Max called.

Guiltily, Kiley got to her feet. "Not yet. How about you?"

"I found the train set I got for my eighth birthday. Maybe we could use it in one of the displays."

Kiley laughed. "I guess one excuse for playing with it is as good as another." She turned to a huge steamer trunk. Opening it, she sniffed as the faint scent of crushed lavender engulfed her. It was a smell reminiscent of long ago and far away, when life was much simpler. Pushing aside the two quilts on top, she peered beneath to find a stack of neatly folded silk garments. She picked one up and discovered it was a pair of cream silk knickers. Holding them up against herself, she squinted at her hazy reflection in an antique mirror on a bureau. Delving into the trunk, she found a matching top. Made of the same cream silk and trimmed with the same hand-crocheted lace, it was cut like a vest with tattered silk ribbons still threaded through the eyelets in front.

Kiley frowned, trying to decide exactly what it was. She turned back to the trunk and almost immediately had her answer when she discovered a corset. The vest was a corset cover. Disbelievingly, she studied the stiff yellowed garment with its long whalebones. She draped it over the trunk lid and delved deeper, this time finding a fragile-looking white lawn dress.

Kiley held the long dress against her and twirled, watching the full skirt billow. She looked around for Max. He was at the other end of the attic shifting boxes.

He wouldn't mind if she tried the clothes on, she decided. She had seen no sign that he was a possessive man. At least not about things.

Stepping behind a box that screened her from Max's vision, she quickly stripped off her clothes. For a moment, she considered trying on the whole outfit just to see what it was like, but one of the whalebones in the corset was broken, and it dug sharply into her rib cage when she held it up, so she tossed it into the trunk. As she pulled on the knickers, a smile of sensual pleasure curved her lips at the feel of the soft silk slithering over her skin. She slipped on the sleeveless vest, shivering slightly as the silk dragged across the sensitive points of her breasts.

Kiley gently tugged on the frayed ribbons, trying to pull the material together, but the edges wouldn't meet. She studied the way her breasts strained against the thin silk in bemusement. Whoever had owned this garment had been the next best thing to flat-chested, she realized, enjoying the unexpectedly voluptuous feeling of spilling out of her underwear.

"No wonder my great-grandfather fathered eight children, if my great-grandmother wandered around looking like that."

Kiley whirled at the sound of Max's husky voice.

"Max! I was just playing dress up." She gestured toward the lawn dress.

"I have a much better idea," he said softly. "Let's play undress."

Kiley's heart stopped for a fraction of a second then lurched into a slow, heavy beat that reverberated through her suddenly tense body.

She stared into his face, watching in awe as it hardened with the force of what he was feeling—desire for her. Exultation bubbled through her at the thought. He might not love her as she did him, but the desire he felt for her was an almost tangible entity vibrating between them. She closed her eyes, allowing the force of his desire to flow over her, feeding her own feelings.

"I've never played undress before. What are the rules of the game?" Kiley swayed toward him, her scantily clad body an irresistible enticement. She intended to use every means at her disposal to strengthen the bond between them.

"Haven't you heard?" His eyes flickered with tiny dancing lights. "There are no rules in love and war."

A fierce longing filled Kiley. A longing for his words to mean he loved her.

"Well, if we're playing undress, I think I win." Kiley twirled, deliberately flaunting her half-naked state. "Because if you'll notice, I definitely have the least on."

Max's husky chuckle echoed through the attic. "I think that means I win, but in the interests of fair play . . ." He yanked off his tie and carelessly tossed it in the general direction of the open trunk. His shirt quickly followed.

"Don't stop now," she urged. "This is just getting interesting."

"No, it got interesting the moment I met you." Max stepped closer to her. "It got out of hand the moment I kissed you."

"Oh?" Her word was a mere whisper of sound.

"Uh-huh."

She watched in mesmerized fascination as he slowly unzipped his pants and let them fall to the floor.

Kiley moistened her dry lips at the sight of his manhood straining against his black briefs.

"Games are played in pairs," Max said softly, and Kiley's fingers obediently plucked at the drawstring holding the knickers up, her attention focused on the slow descent of his briefs. She finally managed to untie the bow, and the knickers fell to her ankles in a slither of silk.

Max reached for her, pulling her against his hard body. Slipping an arm under her hips, he lifted her until her breasts were on a level with his face.

Under his scorching scrutiny, her breasts grew hot, aching for his touch. Kiley gasped as his mouth nuzzled her through the thin silk of the vest. Pleasure so intense it was almost painful shot through her as his mouth latched onto one aching nipple and strongly sucked on it.

Kiley's hands instinctively went to his head to hold him tightly against her. She thrust her fingers into his thick hair and arched against his supporting arm. A tormented moan bubbled out of her throat.

"Max, I want..." She struggled to produce a lucid sentence.

Max raised his head and looked at her breasts. A damp spot encircled one taut, thrusting nipple, and a sensual smile curved his lips. "I can feel what you want... What I want..." he murmured. He studied her other breast and Kiley felt her abdomen clench in anticipation.

"Yes, oh, yes. Please." She tugged his head toward her, caught up in an agony of longing.

"I aim to please," Max whispered against her soft curves and the warmth from his breath heated the silk. Slowly, as if he felt none of the sense of urgency consuming her, he began to lick the other silk-clad nipple.

Kiley dug her fingers into his broad shoulders. Bracing herself, she wrapped her legs around his waist. A sense of exultation filled her as she felt a shudder slam through his body. She could feel him thrusting against her, and suddenly she lost all patience. She wanted him. Now. Needed him within her with a compulsion that overrode rational thought.

"Max!" she demanded imperiously. "I want you." She squirmed against his chest.

"Then you shall have me." Grasping her buttocks, he slowly raised her slightly, then slowly, ever so slowly, pushed her down onto the hot, blunt length of him.

Kiley arched her head and tightened her legs around his waist, forcing him even deeper inside her. His mouth clamped over her throbbing breast and he sucked, sending a jolt of desire coiling through her loins.

"Max!" she wailed. "I can't stand this anymore! I'm coming apart inside."

"Let it happen," Max urged. "I'll catch you." His fingers clenched her hips, each separate finger burning into her feverish skin. Holding her, he forced her first up then down, while the coil of tension tightened its grip on her to unbearable levels.

Kiley clutched frantically at the tight black curls covering his broad chest, her fingertips digging into the damp skin beneath. Her need had become a living thing that demanded satisfaction.

Suddenly, the tension snapped and her whole body clenched with a pleasure that was beyond anything she'd ever felt.

As if on another plane, she felt Max's body convulse in ecstasy, but she was too limp to do more than press loving kisses against his sweat-slick shoulder.

"Thank you for the most fantastic experience of my life, Max Winthrop," she whispered against his throat.

"You're welcome, Kiley Sheridan." He chuckled and his body moved against hers, setting off residual sparks of desire. "You're very welcome." He allowed her to slowly slide down the length of his body to the floor.

Disoriented, Kiley stumbled slightly as she tried to stand and Max scooped her into his arms and sat on the chaise longue with her.

Kiley snuggled her face against his chest, smiling at the way his crisp body hair tickled her nose. Discovering a flat nipple buried in the dark cloud, she probed it with a fingertip.

"Don't do that." His hand closed over hers. "Or we'll never get back to work, and I've got a meeting in . . ." He checked his watch. "An hour and ten minutes."

She sighed voluptuously. "Pity, but that wasn't what I was thinking about. I was actually wondering what this gorgeous old chaise longue was doing in the attic."

"This one?" Max peered at it. "It's haunted."

"Haunted!" Kiley tipped her head and stared into his bright blue eyes, searching for a teasing glint. She couldn't find one. "By what?" she finally asked.

"Not what, whom. My Great-uncle Lucien. He used to lie on this thing and drink himself senseless. He died on it."

"Poor soul." Kiley's soft heart was touched. "How old was he?"

"Ninety-eight."

"Ninety-eight!" Kiley repeated incredulously. "I think you made a mistake. The alcohol didn't kill him—it preserved him."

Max laughed. "Not from my Great-aunt Margaret's wrath. From what I remember as a boy, she was always either yelling at him or trying to drag him to some meeting or other."

"But why blame the chaise longue because the old gentleman finally died?"

"He wasn't a gentleman. He was a reprobate. Anyway, one night about a month after his funeral my Aunt Bea went into his room and saw him lying on the chaise longue grinning at her. And my Aunt Bea is one of the least imaginative women I know."

"So you banished the chair to the attic?"

"No, my mother did because I saw him."

"You did?" she asked skeptically.

"With God as my witness." Kiley felt the shiver that coursed through him. "I was just a kid and I wanted to see a ghost. Any ghost would have done, but I really liked my Uncle Lucien. He used to let me drink the foam off his beer when my parents weren't looking."

"Definitely a reprobate," she said.

"So I took to hanging out in Uncle Lucien's room, and one night I saw him." Kiley felt a cold tremor chase over her skin at his absorbed expression. Max really believed what he was saying. "The longue was sitting in the moonlight and there was a shimmering silvery light on it. I could just make out Uncle Lucien's features, but when I tried to talk to him my mother heard me."

"Didn't she see him?"

"Unfortunately, as she came into the room, she flipped on the light and Uncle Lucien disappeared. As did the chaise longue after I told her about it," Max said ruefully.

"I sure hope the old boy isn't still haunting it."

"Why? My Uncle Lucien would never knowingly hurt anyone. Dead or alive."

"Maybe not, but we could have just shocked the old boy out of his ectoplasm."

Max grinned at her. "Not my Uncle Lucien. But enough about the family skeletons. We need to get back to the store." He tipped her off his lap.

"Did you find the animals?" Kiley reached for her clothes.

"Uh-huh. I'll send a truck and a couple of men out to pick them up. They look to be in pretty good shape, and speaking of shapes . . ." He watched as she pulled her panties on.

"You're the one who wants to go back to the store," she reminded him, elated by the hot glow in his eyes.

"Has to go back," he corrected. "Why don't you take that old lingerie with you and we can try it out some other time. Better still, I'll have the men who pick up the animals take a couple of these old trunks to your house. Who knows what we might find in them." His features hardened as his eyes lingered on the swollen fullness of her breasts.

"Who knows indeed," she added huskily, encouraged by his casual willingness to entrust her with his family's possessions and by his assumption that their relationship would be stretching into the foreseeable future.

THAT KNOWLEDGE gave her a feeling of hope that carried her through the rest of the week. To her infinite relief, nothing more was stolen, and Kiley found herself beginning to relax, hoping that the rash of thefts had come to an end. Her tentative attempts to discover the thief had been unsuccessful. She didn't have the experience or the resources to investigate anything other than an educational topic.

Unfortunately, her optimism proved unwarranted. On Friday the situation blew up in her face.

Kiley was in the employees' lunch room with Jane when Jane suddenly pointed toward the door and asked, "Isn't that our exalted leader?"

Kiley turned to look, and a warm feeling of pleasure engulfed her at the sight of Max. She waved at him, but uncertainly lowered her hand when there was no answering smile.

"I wonder what happened," Jane said. "He looks like he just ran afoul of the IRS."

"Maybe he found your grow light and he's coming for retribution?" Kiley tried to dislodge the sinking feeling in the pit of her stomach with a joke.

"Not a chance." Jane nodded toward the oversize purse lying at her feet. "I carry the evidence with me."

"No wonder he can't find it."

Jane giggled. "But he's having such fun looking."

"Kiley." Max's voice was harsh, and she swallowed uneasily. It was fast becoming clear that something was very wrong.

"Max." She forced a smile that wavered slightly when confronted with the continued bleakness of his expression. "What's wrong?"

"There's a problem with one of your students and I'd like you to come along with me. Excuse us, Jane."

Kiley dropped her napkin on her half-eaten lunch and hurriedly got to her feet.

"Which one?" she asked as she lengthened her stride to keep up with him.

"Amad. I told you I wouldn't act without evidence, and now I've got it. Acton's in my office with Amad, and he has proof that the kid's been stealing."

"I'll believe Amad is guilty of theft when he tells me so and not a minute before," Kiley said vehemently.

"We'll discuss this when we get to my office."

"Are we going to have a discussion or are you going to simply react?" She grabbed his arm to make him listen to her.

Max stared into her pleading face as frustration and anger coursed through him. Frustration that he couldn't give her what she wanted and anger that Amad had betrayed her trust.

"Kiley, listen to me. Acton has proof that Amad stole from the store."

"And if it's valid then I understand your feeling that you have no choice but to fire Amad. All I'm asking is that you listen to Amad's side of the story before you do anything. I know him. He wouldn't steal."

"I'll listen," Max promised, glad to be able to give her some small comfort in all this mess.

With a shaky smile at the worried-looking Aggie, Kiley followed Max into his office. Amad was sitting in a chair in front of Max's desk looking shell-shocked. A vaguely familiar man was leaning against the far wall. She recognized him as being from security. Acton, she assumed, when Max forgot to introduce him to her.

"Miss Sheridan." Acton nodded at her. "It was good of you to come."

Kiley purposefully walked over and stood by Amad, making her sympathies quite clear.

"What's the problem, Amad?" Kiley asked.

"He—" Amad nodded to Acton "—says that I stole that." Amad pointed toward a bracelet lying on the desk beside a battered-looking gym bag she recognized as belonging to Amad.

Kiley picked up the slender chain of diamonds, watching as the light was refracted off the gems.

"Is it real?" Amad's voice broke, and Kiley caught a glimpse of the fear he was trying so hard to hide.

Kiley shrugged. "I'm no expert, but I'd assume so. I mean, what's the point of stealing rhinestones?"

"It's real," Max clipped out. "About two thousand dollars worth of real."

Amad turned to Max. "I didn't take it, Mr. Winthrop."

"We found it in your gym bag," Acton said.

"Which was probably being kept in your locker up in the employee lounge?" Kiley asked Amad.

He nodded.

"Which anyone could have gotten into," Kiley pointed out. "Good Lord, my first day here I watched someone open a locker with a credit card."

Acton grimaced. "A lamentable habit."

"But a widespread one," Kiley insisted.

"True," Max conceded, and Kiley breathed a sigh of relief at the admission. If she could just get him thinking instead of reacting . . .

"Tell me, Mr. Acton," she asked, "why did you search Amad's stuff?"

"Why?" Acton looked confused.

"I mean, have you been looking through his things every day? Or did someone tip you off that you'd find that bracelet in his bag? Someone who might be trying to set him up?"

"Who'd do that?" Amad seemed more upset by the idea of having been gullible than by being thought a thief. "Everybody's been real nice—" he gulped "—until now."

"Nobody gave us any tips," Acton said. "We asked jewelry to keep a very close eye on things after that watch disappeared last Saturday. They discovered the bracelet missing about half an hour ago."

"And you immediately searched through Amad's stuff. It doesn't even sound legal," she accused.

"Yes, it is," Acton broke in.

"Oh, I signed something that said they could," Amad told her. "When we was orientated. I mean, what did I care. I wasn't planning on stealing nothing, and I didn't," he insisted. "Hell, fencing hot jewelry is no way to make a quick score. The only one that makes much profit on that is the fence."

"That so?" Acton eyed him speculatively.

"Yeah, that's so!" Amad said belligerently. "Everybody in my neighborhood knows that if you want to make a bundle fast, selling drugs is the way to go."

"Hmm." Max eyed the boy thoughtfully.

"So, what you're saying, Mr. Acton, is that it was your idea to go through Amad's things. You weren't acting on a tip," Kiley continued.

"Yes," Acton said. "According to the jewelry supervisor, Amad was in the department for a few minutes at about eleven."

"I only stopped by on my way to Miss Sheridan's class to tell David that I'd be able to go," Amad defended himself.

"Go?" Max queried.

"To his house after work to swim," Amad said. "He asked me yesterday, and I wasn't sure I could, so he said to let him know today. So I did."

"Ah, yes. The ubiquitous David." Kiley turned to Max. "Hasn't it struck you as strange that David pops up every single time something happens?"

"David's my friend!" Amad was outraged. "He'd never set me up."

Max let his breath out on a long sigh. "Strange, but not conclusive. The bracelet was found on Amad."

"No, it was found in Amad's gym bag, which is not the same thing at all. I never claimed that David was stupid. If I was going to steal something, I sure wouldn't want to risk carrying it out of the store myself."

"She's got a point there," Acton conceded. "It certainly is risky."

"And what better way to transport the bracelet than to invite Amad to come swimming? He brings his bag with his gear to work, David lets himself into Amad's locker with a credit card, stashes the loot in the bag and retrieves it later at his house. Amad would never suspect a thing."

"Amad had that bag at the house when your clock was stolen," Max said reflectively.

"I didn't take no clock. I didn't take nothin'!" Amad's voice rose in bitter frustration. "And I can prove it. I want a lie detector test."

"No, you don't," Kiley said swiftly.

"But—" Amad began.

"She's right," Max told him. "Lie detectors are notoriously unreliable. Simply being nervous and angry about all this could create a guilty reading. That's why we never use the things."

"But I didn't take nothin'," Amad persisted.

"I'm going to look into this a little more, Amad," Max said, ignoring Acton's protest. "I want you to go back to sporting goods. Don't say anything about the bracelet to anyone until we get to the bottom of this."

"But David—" Amad began.

"To anyone," Max clipped out. "If you won't give me your word, then I'll have Mr. Acton escort you off the store premises and you'll stay off them until I can unravel this mess."

The fact that Max seemed willing to accept his word tipped the balance. With a grudging consent, Amad left.

"Max, I know Miss Sheridan thinks he's innocent, but for God's sake we found the stolen item secreted in his things," Acton protested.

"Rather conveniently, don't you think?" Max asked slowly. "Kiley makes a good point. It would have been much safer for David to use Amad to carry the stuff out, and he could easily recover it tonight. It does seem a little strange that he would just happen to invite Amad to go swimming the night something is stolen again."

"You actually think David Mallings stole that bracelet?" Acton asked incredulously.

Max rubbed the back of his neck in frustration. "I don't know. I don't know anything about David except that his father's a very good friend of mine and one of the best vice presidents we've ever had."

"What do you know about Amad?" Action countered.

Max studied Kiley thoughtfully for a few seconds, then said, "Not much more, but Kiley knows him. Has known him for four years, and she says he's honest. And the kid makes one very relevant point," Max added. "If he wanted to make money illegally, selling drugs would be a whole lot easier and much more profitable than shoplifting."

"So now what?" Acton asked.

"Now I think we talk to David. Would you ask him to come up?" Max said.

Kiley waited until Acton left, then said, "Thank you, Max."

Max grimaced. "Don't thank me yet. I'm not convinced that Amad didn't do it. It's just that it doesn't quite add up. But why would David steal? Jim has plenty of money and David's an only child. Hell!" Max got up and began to pace across his office in frustration. "Jim even bought him a new Ferrari when he graduated last month."

"Perhaps he has expenses he doesn't want his dad to know about?" Kiley guessed. "David himself doesn't make all that much money and he's only been working a week longer than Amad. Maybe . . . maybe he has a girlfriend who's expensive?"

"Kiley, he could support a Washington call girl on what's been stolen recently," Max said wryly.

"Well . . . perhaps his girlfriend's pregnant. Perhaps he doesn't want to tell his father..." She paused as Max shook his head.

"His parents would be in seventh heaven at the thought of a grandchild. They wouldn't ask and wouldn't care about the circumstances."

"All right," Kiley conceded. "So I'm a little weak on motivation, but—" She broke off as Acton returned with David.

A nervous David. Kiley's eyes narrowed as she studied the pallor of his skin and the way his gaze skittered away from hers.

"You wanted to see me, Mr. Winthrop?" David asked.

"Yes." Max nodded toward the chair Amad had been sitting in. "Please sit down. We have a slight problem we're hoping you can help us with."

"If I can." David seemed to gain confidence at Max's words.

"It's about that." Max nodded toward the diamond bracelet on the desk.

David picked it up, and Kiley could see the very faint tremor in his fingers as he did so. Guilt? Or simply nerves at being the focal point of three adults, one of whom owned the store and another who was the head of security?

David gave it a cursory glance then replaced it on the desk. "It's one of ours, isn't it?"

"We found it in Amad's gym bag. He was in your department this morning," Max said.

"But Amad was with me the whole time he was there. I didn't see him take it." David's voice shook slightly, and Kiley felt a surge of pity. She was becoming more convinced by the second that David had used Amad, but it obviously hadn't been done with malice.

"There's another answer," Acton offered. "I checked with your supervisor. You took your morning break after Amad was there, but before she noticed the bracelet was gone."

"Did you take it, David?" Kiley asked softly.

"Answer Miss Sheridan, David." Jim Mallings spoke from the doorway.

"Dad!" David seemed to pale even more. "What are you doing here?"

"I saw you pass by my office with Acton and I was curious about why the two of you would be going to see Max. Now answer Miss Sheridan. Did you steal that thing?" He gestured disdainfully at the glittering bracelet.

"Dad, I—"

"Did you take it?" Jim demanded.

David stared at him for a second, took a deep breath then blurted, "Yes. Amad didn't have a clue about what I was doing."

"But why?" Jim's voice cracked.

"Because I had to have the money," David muttered.

"Why?" Jim repeated.

"Because . . . because last year at a party after a basketball game one of the guys passed around some stuff that he said was a great high," David said as if relieved to be finally saying it.

"And you took some?" Jim seemed to age before Kiley's eyes.

David half turned as if he couldn't bear to see the stark pain etched on his father's face.

"I'd been smoking marijuana for years and it hadn't hurt me any," David muttered defensively. "I figured I could control the cocaine, too. And at first I could, but . . . it kept taking more and more of the stuff to get high and I never seemed to have enough money and I could hardly ask you for it, could I?" David's smile was a travesty. "I was desperate—you have no idea what it's like. Finally the guy I was buying from said he'd trade if I could bring him things."

"My clock," Kiley said.

David gave her a quick, shamed glance. "He didn't like it. He said he wanted small items like watches and jewelry. I was afraid to risk getting it back to you so I hid it in my closet."

Jim straightened his shoulders and said, "I'll return it to you tomorrow, Miss Sheridan, when I hand in my resignation."

"No!" Max barked. "Absolutely not, Jim. You have a contract with this store, and I refuse to release you from it."

Jim looked at Max incredulously. "But you can't want me working for you after . . ." He gestured impotently at David's hunched figure.

"You're exactly the same person now as you were before this happened," Max said.

"But David—"

"Made a very bad error in judgement," Max said, "and unfortunately it's a mistake a lot of young adults are making these days. The important thing now is getting him some help to overcome it."

"I'm sorry, Dad." David gulped and looked away. "I never meant to hurt anyone. I wanted to stop, but I couldn't."

"We'll help." His father pulled him against his chest and hugged him. "Your mother and I love you. This doesn't make any difference to how we feel. We'll solve this problem together. Let's go home and call Dr. Knowlton and ask him for a referral to a treatment center."

Jim turned to Max and said, "If you'll let me know the cost of what he . . . stole, I'll write the store a check. When you process his dismissal papers, would—"

"Addiction is a disease, Jim," Max said, "and that's the way we'll treat it. We'll put David on medical leave and he can decide what he wants to do when he's licked this thing."

"No!" David looked panicky. "If you do that, everyone will know—"

"How about if we say you unexpectedly got a great job offer, and since retailing wasn't turning out to be as interesting as you thought, you grabbed the chance," Kiley suggested. "You certainly won't be the first to jump ship. Wayland's already handed in his resignation."

"And later, if you want to return, you can say you changed your mind," Max added with an approving look at Kiley.

"Thanks, Mr. Winthrop," David said. "And I'm sorry about everything. I will beat it. I will."

"Of course you will," Kiley said. "And while you're working on it, why don't you drop a line to Amad every once in a while and let him know how you're doing."

David grimaced. "After what I did? He won't want to hear from me."

"Amad will understand," Kiley said. "He knows what drugs can drive a man to do. He sees it every day in his own neighborhood."

"But I used him."

"True, but when push came to shove, you didn't let him take the blame," Kiley said seriously. "Loyalty means a lot to Amad."

"Tell him..." David shook his head. "Just tell him I'm sorry."

"I will," Kiley assured him as Jim put his arm around his son's shoulder and urged him out of the office.

Acton followed them out. Max silently closed the door behind them and stood blindly staring at it.

"God, I wish this were the twenty-second century," Kiley exploded.

"What?" Max turned and stared uncomprehendingly at her.

"And we had space travel and we could put all the monsters who prey on kids like that on an isolated planet and let them destroy each other."

"Shades of Botany Bay." Max opened his arms and Kiley rushed into the haven they promised. She slipped her arms inside his suit jacket and snuggled against him, drawing warmth from his body. Warmth to help melt the sense of impotent frustration she felt.

She sighed unhappily. "I feel so awful, Max. I wanted Amad proved innocent but . . . That poor kid. And his parents . . ."

"David'll make it," Max said emphatically as if willing it to be true. "And you were right. The only thing Amad was guilty of was bad judgment." He grimaced. "As I was, and I don't even have the excuse of being eighteen."

"Well, you don't know Amad like I do, and at least you didn't act rashly."

"Speaking of acting rashly . . ." Max stared into her upturned face.

"What's the matter?" Kiley asked.

"I'm trying to decide whether to act rashly or try a more conservative approach. The problem is that with you in my arms acting rashly comes so naturally."

"I think I prefer the term spontaneous." Kiley watched in fascination as the dark center of his pupils expanded under the force of the emotion gripping him. "In fact, you give a whole new meaning to the term spontaneity." She wiggled closer to his hardening body as she suddenly realized that Amad's supposed involvement in the thefts no longer loomed between them. Now she could revel in their developing relationship without fear of what might happen.

"Well, if you like spontaneous..." Max stared at her, took a deep breath and said, "Let's run away to Nevada and get married."

"What!" Kiley stared at him in shock.

"You said you like spontaneous," he accused.

"I do. I mean . . ."

He stiffened. "Then it must be me you object to."

The uncertainty in his eyes was all Kiley needed. Max was never uncertain, even when he was wrong. If he was uncertain now, it had to be because her answer was vitally important to him. She was vitally important to him.

Deciding that nothing would serve but total honesty, Kiley met his gaze and said, "I love you, Max Winthrop." She watched as his beloved face registered first shock then incredulous joy.

"My darling, darling woman." He crushed her to him in an embrace that made it difficult to breathe. "I love you, love you, love you," he chanted. He relaxed his hold slightly and demanded, "Then you'll elope to Las Vegas with me?"

"Sure." Kiley grinned ecstatically at him. "I get off work at five."

"Which reminds me of something I've been meaning to talk to you about," Max said slowly.

"My getting off work?"

"No, the work you've been doing here. Your idea of finding your students jobs was sound, but I think you're going about it backward."

"Oh?" Kiley murmured, her attention on the movement of his lips as he talked. She wanted to feel those lips against hers, not listen to the words they were shaping.

"Yes, what we ought to do is to start them out part-time their junior year. Then we could gradually ease them into regular jobs when they graduate. I've discussed the idea with several other area business people and most are willing to hire a couple of your kids after they've served a successful apprenticeship with us. You could run the program full time. You'd do a lot more good in that role than teaching, and if you're here in the store you'd be close enough for frequent breaks." His eyes glowed with promise.

Kiley heaved a sigh of pure, undiluted happiness, and said, "I love you Max Winthrop."

"And I love you, soon-to-be Mrs. Max Winthrop," he whispered against her softly parted lips.

It was the last coherent thought either of them had for a long time.

# THE LOVES OF A CENTURY...

Join American Romance in a nostalgic look back at the Twentieth Century—at the lives and loves of American men and women from the turn-of-the-century to the dawn of the year 2000.

Journey through the decades from the dance halls of the 1900s to the discos of the seventies ... from Glenn Miller to the Beatles ... from Valentino to Newman ... from corset to miniskirt ... from beau to Significant Other.

Relive the moments ... recapture the memories.

Look now for the CENTURY OF AMERICAN ROMANCE series in Harlequin American Romance. In one of the four American Romance titles appearing each month, for the next twelve months, we'll take you back to a decade of the Twentieth Century, where you'll relive the years and rekindle the romance of days gone by.

Don't miss a day of the CENTURY OF AMERICAN ROMANCE.

The women...the men...the passions...
the memories....

CAR-1